SOMETIMES ONLY THE SAD SONGS WILL DO

Sometimes Only the Sad Songs Will Do

short stories by

David Denny

Shanti Arts Publishing

Brunswick, Maine

SOMETIMES ONLY THE SAD SONGS WILL DO

Published by Shanti Arts Publishing
Cover and interior design by Shanti Arts Designs

Shanti Arts LLC
Brunswick, Maine

www.shantiarts.com

Cover image: *Walking Man* is by Max Hammond
and is used with his permission.
www.maxhammond.net

Printed in the United States of America

ISBN: 978-1-951651-38-1 (softcover)
ISBN: 978-1-951651-39-8 (digital)

Library of Congress Control Number: 202094289

In loving memory of my father, Mahlon Denny,
who cherished the sad songs,
and my mother, Patricia Denny,
who sang along with the happy songs,
and to my sister, Susan Johnson,
who remembers with me the warmth of
a home filled with music.

There's a lover in the story,
but the story's still the same.
There's a lullaby for suffering
and a paradox to blame.
It's written in the scriptures;
it's not some idle claim.
You want it darker?
We kill the flame.

— Leonard Cohen

You have to cherish the world
at the same time that you
struggle to endure it.

— Flannery O'Connor

CONTENTS

Sometimes Only the Sad Songs Will Do

WE HAD SOME TROUBLE HERE LAST WEEK. YOU MAY HAVE heard about it. If you watch the local news, then you for sure heard about it. You saw a picture of me, though you might not have known it was me at the time, and I was seated in the back of a sheriff's cruiser, my hands in cuffs and a bloody open wound on my left cheek. You may remember the studio news reporter using words like *homeless* and *deranged* and *dangerous*. I am none of those things. But those labels made for an entertaining *Eyewitness News* moment, didn't they? I don't know who writes the news, but I know they aren't much interested in subtlety. Certainly truth rarely enters into it. But then, as Pilate said to Christ on the morning of his execution, "What is truth?"

Last Thursday I was out walking. I've been walking a lot lately. I call it walk therapy. I started walk therapy soon after giving up talk therapy. I gave up talk therapy because it didn't seem to be helping and because I'm pretty sure my therapist was talking to my father behind my back. I'll tell you why. He began all friendly and sympathetic. Who doesn't need a friendly and sympathetic listener? That was enough to hook me. But after a few sessions he started to act and sound just like my father, who has a great deal in common with Hermann Kafka.

A good therapist is supposed to guide you gently toward healing and self-discovery. My therapist listened for a while, and then he started growing irritated and impatient with me, just like my father. Soon he put down his notebook and crossed his arms on his chest. And then he began asking questions that, make no mistake, weren't actually questions at all. My father too has this annoying habit of posing criticism *in the form of questions.* For example, my father once crossed his arms just so and said, "You're essentially a lazy person, aren't you?" One of his favorite pseudo-questions goes like this: "You think the world owes you a living, don't you?"

And so, after a honeymoon period of three sessions, during which the therapist listened intently and jotted notes, on our fourth meeting he abandoned the notebook altogether. He leaned back and clasped his hands behind his head, an unconscious father gesture if ever there was one, and said, "What's stopping you from getting a job?" The final straw came in the next session when he stood and poured himself a cup of coffee right as I was telling him about how Margo used to punch me in my sleep. He said, "You whine a lot, have you noticed that?" I politely thanked him for his service and told him he could expect a nice, fat check in the mail from my father. That marked the end of my talk therapy and the beginning of my walk therapy.

Well, so, I was out walking. I had my earbuds in, listening to the Cowboy Junkies. Oh, so that's another thing the therapist said to me. "Why don't you listen to happy music? Maybe the Cowboy Junkies are only giving you permission to feel miserable." As psychotherapy, that part is not so far-fetched. It was the next thing he said that crossed over the therapeutic line: "And when you feel miserable, you make everyone else miserable, don't you?"

What some people don't seem to understand is that sometimes only the sad songs will do. There are times when happy songs don't make you happy; they only mock your inability to *be* happy. Half the book of Psalms are poems of lament. There's good reason for that: this life is hard, brother. And quite often it just doesn't make any sense. Singing a happy tune in the face of such misery is ludicrous. If I had my wits about me (but when do I ever?), I might've said back to the therapist, "Wouldn't you say singing happy tunes in the face of misery is, well, ludicrous?" On further reflection, I'm pretty sure the word *ludicrous* is too sharp in tone to achieve the intended effect. My retort might be better phrased, "Wouldn't you say singing happy tunes in the face of misery is a diversion into magical thinking?" If my experience last week has taught me anything, it is the value of rhetorical accuracy.

So there I was out walking last Thursday with the Cowboy Junkies in my ears. The other thing about the Cowboy Junkies is that the lead singer is named Margo. I just discovered that by accident one day. I was scrolling through some of their albums when her picture and name popped up. She looks nothing like my Margo. But there she was singing these sad songs in my ear, and all along she had the same name as my dead girlfriend.

Well, so, there's no way you could know this part of the story, so I might as well tell you. Last September my girlfriend, Margo, was out walking our dog, Patch, next to the golf course. She was hit by lightning. There was a foursome standing nearby beneath a tree, and they saw the whole thing.

It had been raining off and on all day, and during one of the off periods Margo leashed up Patch and took him out. I don't know why she didn't take cover like the golfers, except that she loved walking in the rain. And Patch didn't seem to mind it either. There were two strikes about a quarter mile away, which is why the foursome had taken cover.

The bolt hit her in the right shoulder, driving her straight to the ground. The golfers noted the odor—a sharp, bitter smell, like sulfur, which the Bible calls *brimstone*. One of them told the news reporter he saw a puff of smoke rise off her sweater. Patch took off running into the woods. I never found him. I have a bizarre inkling as to his fate, but I'll save that for later.

Well, so, there I was listening to this other Margo in my ear and walking—walking not so far, in fact, from the golf course, on the warmest day of the hot spell last week. And I'd been smoking a little weed that morning. So I have my walking therapy and I sometimes combine that with my smoking therapy. I saw a documentary recently about Louis Armstrong, saying that he smoked a joint every morning of his life. It seemed to work for him. He's the guy famous for, among many others, the classic rendition of "What a Wonderful World," a happy song if ever there was one, a song that celebrates natural beauty and simplicity—important goals of my walk therapy.

So I admit I was lightly baked that morning. But when the news reporter described me as "under the influence of a controlled substance," she was being deliberately vague, suggesting I might have been coked up. She provided this information just after she used the word *deranged*, among others, to differentiate me from the Good Samaritan who had called the cops. Every story needs a hero. In the parable of the Good Samaritan, it's the Samaritan, hence the journalistic cliché.

So there I was, walking along near the golf course when I smelled a strong, musky odor. And I thought maybe there must be a dead dog or a dead deer in the bushes. Cars are always hitting animals on this particular stretch because there are no streetlights. Also, the road curves there near the creek and then climbs quickly up a steep grade as the woods thicken. People are always taking that curve too fast. You can hear the brakes squeal all the way over at our place. Sorry, my place. The place I lived for two years with Margo. The place where now the toilet seats are permanently left up and the sink is always cluttered with unwashed dishes. So I smelled this smell, a pretty powerful, disgusting odor, and I started to look around.

The bushes were clear except for a few candy wrappers and soda cans. But the smell was stronger than ever. I couldn't shake it. You might be thinking it was probably a skunk. But I know skunk odor, and this was different.

For some reason I looked up into this old sycamore tree. Did I hear something up there? I don't recall. But there, laid out across a thick horizontal branch, was a mountain lion. He was stretched out up there, sleeping.

I wasn't afraid. I was in a mellow state of mind. I didn't feel a rush of adrenaline. Instead, I was fascinated. I stood there looking up. This was a big cat. The news people later said he was a two-hundred-pounder, and six feet long, from nose to tail. I'm not saying I'm brave. Far from it. I'm sure my calmness was encouraged by the weed. But also I just didn't feel threatened. Mountain lion attacks are rare, says *Wikipedia*. They prefer deer to humans any day. In fact, you're more likely to get hit by lightning than be attacked by a mountain lion. Thanks, *Wikipedia*. No, the irony of that statement is not lost on me.

He was asleep, all right. While I was watching him, one of his paws twitched, and his black-tipped tail moved in a kind of slow sweep. I shuffled around to where I could see him better. In fact, I wasn't really watching where I was going, and it turns out I stepped into the street. I guess I was standing there, shading my eyes, just gazing at this wild creature. Really, I've never seen anything more beautiful. Two hundred pounds of tawny muscle. I wish you could've seen it. But thanks to the Good Samaritan in the Tesla, you never will. When her brakes squealed and she jumped from her car to yell at me, the lion awoke.

The Tesla lady hadn't seen the cat. She was too busy calling the cops on her cell phone. She didn't like the looks of me. Not one bit. And I was blocking her way. Into her phone, she said, "Yes, this *is* an emergency!"

Coming the opposite direction, a pickup truck loaded with landscaping tools eased to a stop. As it turned out, I was standing out on the yellow line. The Mexican guy in the truck also got out of his vehicle, but he was calm enough to notice the direction I was staring. He spotted the lion. "Holy shit," he said, "is that thing for real?" He sidled up next to me and adjusted his Giants cap so he could get a better look. "Are you fucking kidding me?" he said.

The lion was fully awake now. He yawned and stretched, showing his teeth and clawing the branch. The odor was even stronger than before.

Then the Tesla lady looked up and let out a bloodcurdling cry. She screamed and screamed.

You might say I acted on instinct. All I wanted was to stop the screaming. I clamped my hand over Tesla lady's mouth and tried to shove her back inside her car. Maybe I dragged her a little bit because one of her high heels snapped off on the asphalt.

She struggled, of course. It may have looked like we were tangling. At some point her string of pearls broke and scattered all over the roadway. Apparently, too, she had a bruise in the shape of my hand on her upper arm. On the news you may have seen a close-up photo of that arm.

But, as I said to the sheriff when he tucked me into the back of his cruiser, I may have saved that woman's life. If I'd been the mountain lion, I'd have broken the neck of anyone making that horrible screeching noise. I should learn to keep my mouth shut. Instead, I played right into their narrative.

Tesla lady's real name is Sheryl Liu, and she's the top broker for a prominent real estate team here in Silicon Valley. Ms. Liu accused me, among other things, of racism. How else to explain the violent outburst of a drugged-up, middle-aged white guy? Any good court-appointed psychologist would cite a case of socioeconomic jealousy against the most successful immigrant group in the country. But even Sheryl Liu, in the end, is not as rich and powerful as my father.

It was amazing how fast the cop car arrived: just as the lion was beginning to pace the branch. I covered my ears to mute the siren's cry. The landscaper wisely turned his truck around and drove away. But others arrived—neighbors drawn out of their homes to see what all the racket was about.

The young cop approached me with his Taser drawn. I pointed up into the tree. Clearly agitated, the cat was still pacing back and forth atop the big branch. The cop holstered his Taser and spoke into his shoulder mic: "I need a game warden ASAP."

Now there were half a dozen people standing on the sidewalk. Tesla lady lowered her window and hurled a series of accusations about me. Among the words she shouted were *maniac* and *drug addict*. I must have smelled from the pot I'd smoked. Keeping one eye on the lion, the cop approached me with his hands out to his sides. "I'm not going to have any more trouble with you, am I?"

Just my luck, the sheriff's department dispatched their youngest and most ambitious cop, a decorated Iraq War veteran who had received a special commendation from the mayor during the previous year for writing the most traffic citations. He had also single-handedly stopped a bank robbery in progress at the local Wells Fargo branch. Among city officials, he is known as Robocop. His real name is Richard Beall—that's Deputy Rick Beall to you and me. Remember that name; he's sure to be Governor someday.

He circled around to my right, grabbing one arm and twisting it behind my back. Then he grabbed the other arm. In no time I was face down on the asphalt, and he was cuffing my wrists behind my back. He placed his boot on my neck. It was this face-plant on the asphalt that scrubbed a few layers of skin off my left cheek, creating an impressive patch of blood and loose flesh and road tar. There I was, a made-to-order, incapacitated food source for a wild predator. No effort, no chase. I'm surprised the sheriff didn't just shout up to the lion, "Chow's on!"

It was then that Tesla lady turned her attention to the lion. She pointed into the tree and screamed. Some of the words she formed in her high-pitched squeal were *dangerous* and *diseased*. To this she added *children* and *pets*. As if on cue, the mountain lion leaped from branch to trunk, his great paws springing from the trunk and touching down on the asphalt.

The cop lifted his boot from my throat and drew his firearm.

"Run!" I yelled at the lion.

But the lion was surrounded by cars and gawkers who had formed a circle around the scene. The lion took a step in the direction of the cop. His great tail rose up behind him and swished from side to side. He opened his mouth, revealing long canines, and he made a bloodcurdling cry of his own—not a roar exactly, but a low, raspy yowl of warning.

Everybody backed away except Robocop.

"Shoot!" screamed Tesla lady. "Shoot it!"

"Run!" I yelled.

The cat saw an opening and walked toward it. He sauntered up the middle of the street. Amazing animal. I twisted my torso in an attempt to watch his escape. The cop trained his weapon on the lion as he walked away.

"Shoot!" screamed Tesla lady. "It's your job to protect and defend!"

That, apparently, was all Robocop needed to hear. When he fired his first shot, I turned my head away. In quick succession he fired a second, third, fourth, and fifth bullet. When I looked again, the cop stood over the lion, his gun still aimed at the dead animal. He kicked it.

A brief moment of silence settled over us—over the dead lion and the proud cop, over the Tesla lady, over me, on my belly, bleeding and crying, straddling the double yellow line. Somewhere on the asphalt nearby the muffled sounds of the Cowboy Junkies softly crooned another lament through the tiny speakers in my earbuds.

When the warden's green truck pulled up, he exchanged harsh words with Robocop, words like *protocol* and *impulsive* and (have I just redacted this one for my own purposes?) *ludicrous*. While the warden wrapped the lion in burlap, the cop loaded me into the back of his cruiser. He took the notes that Tesla lady dictated. Everyone else filtered back into the languid business of a hot suburban afternoon.

As I was gazing at the bloodstains on the asphalt—mine and the lion's—the TV crew rolled into place. And that's how the unfortunate footage of me, cuffed in the back of the cop car, ended up playing such a prominent role in that evening's lead story on *Eyewitness News* at six and eleven.

Well, so, my father was able to negotiate my release and convince the Tesla lady to drop the charges against me, under the conditions that I resume talk therapy and spend a month in a locked rehab facility in Napa. It was an expensive foray into TV stardom.

But my father can afford it. Seeing as how Tesla lady was using the words *hate crime*, I'd guess my father was forced to mortgage one of his commercial properties. Between me and the cat, it might've been nice if just one of us had been allowed to go free.

I've had time to reflect, and it's occurred to me that our dog, Patch, was eaten by the mountain lion. The very beast whose freedom I pleaded for ingested our pet, and I'm convinced the only hate crime committed that day was against the wild part inside each of us.

I've been integrating more Louis Armstrong into my playlist. Since I'm no longer allowed my daily cannabis, I'm hoping prolonged exposure to Satchmo will lend me some residual effects by aural osmosis. It turns out most of his songs are just as sad as the Cowboy Junkies'. The sound quality isn't as sharp, due to the more primitive recording equipment back in the day. But the quality of the music itself is what matters. It's all about how the music opens you up inside. Call it a remedy for the hysteria of the postmodern world.

In the parable of the Good Samaritan, the priest and the Levite pass by the fallen man, who lies in a ditch, a bloody mess, having been robbed and beaten and left for dead. They both have their reasons. Only the Samaritan stops to help. By this reckoning, the real hero of this story is not the Tesla lady. Nor is it Robocop. Am I so deluded as to think of myself as the true hero of this story? I know what you're thinking: ludicrous!

Monday Morning

A S BRAD BACKED HIS CAR OUT OF THE GARAGE, HE FELT THE right rear tire rise up slightly and then drop back down. Had there also been some sort of noise? He braked and turned the radio off. He put the car into Park. He might have run over something. He got out of the car and walked around to the passenger side. The black and white fur just beneath the car confirmed it. What was it—a skunk, or . . . no, it was a cat. A big cat. Mort's cat. The one who had taken to sunbathing on the warm concrete of Brad's driveway.

He squatted beside the creature, put his hand on its belly. The torso had contorted a bit, twisted somehow when the tire crushed its midsection, leaving its rear legs pointing upward. He pushed them back down into place, immediately wondering why. Reflex, he guessed. A wave of nausea came over him. The yogurt he'd shoveled into his mouth while watching CNN rose to the back of his throat. He swallowed hard and drew in a slow, deep breath. OK, he could deal with this.

He scooped up the animal.

As he stood, the cat's head and tail drooped over the sides of the cradle he made with his arms. A thick splotch of blood and goo remained on the driveway where the cat's mouth had been. Brad looked around. Had any of the neighbors seen? Surely they were all at work by now. What a nice morning it was—a cool, clear, mid-spring morning with a few clouds hugging the foothills and birds twittering in the privet and plum trees.

He'd killed Mort's cat, and now he'd be late to work. His programming team would have to start without him. He should text them. His cell phone lay on the passenger seat of his car. He glanced at the dead cat in his arms. Silicon Valley ethics dictated you never leave your phone. Too many security breaches occurred from lost or stolen phones. Well, he'd have to leave it. He'd just go drop the cat on Mort's front porch, rinse his hands with the garden hose, and head to the office. He could text his team on the way.

A FEW WEEKS earlier Mort had come to Brad's door. A retired cop, Mort waddled rather than walked because of an old back injury. He rarely left his house, and Brad was surprised to see him standing on his front porch.

"Someone's feeding my cat," Mort said. "I'm just going up and down the block to tell everybody not to feed my cat. I'll be the one to feed him, get me?"

"Sure, Mort," Brad replied. "What's your cat look like? I'll keep an eye out for him."

Mort looked startled to hear Brad use his name. Brad and Mort had held numerous conversations out at the mailboxes in recent years, but Mort was getting older, and each time he saw Brad he seemed to have trouble remembering him. "He can keep an eye on himself. Just don't feed him. He's a big guy, black mostly but with a patch of white on his chest and white spots on his front paws."

"Oh, that's *your* cat?" Brad had seen the cat lurking around the neighborhood and assumed it was a stray. In fact, one day Brad had opened a can of tuna and left it for him with a bowl of water just on the edge of his driveway.

Once again Mort looked startled to hear his name. He eyed Brad suspiciously, as though Brad were a door-to-door solicitor.

Mort lived at the end of the street, across from Carol, an elderly recluse and hoarder. Mort and Carol had lived in this neighborhood longer than anyone else. They went back to the days before the Silicon empires were born. Mort watched out for her; he even picked up her mail, what little there was. Mort had lost his wife to cancer, and he had been known to ramble about a son lost to a drug overdose in the 1970s. In those days the neighborhood was mostly working class, with a few local teachers and Lockheed engineers mixed in.

Carol often left her front door standing wide open—did she just forget to close it behind her?—and anyone could see that it was filled with piles of old newspapers, broken furniture, and discarded toys. Lately she had acquired a sailboat and several bicycles with missing parts that were stacked precariously in her side yard, fully visible from the street. Brad wondered if he should call someone. He'd heard that Carol had an estranged daughter. Brad had considered tracking her down, just to let her know that the situation was getting to be, well, out of control. But then, really, what business was it of his? He just lived on this street.

"He's my cat," Mort said. "I'm just going around telling everybody." He turned to leave.

"Right, OK. How've you been, Mort?"

"Oh," he gazed out at the street, "I feel about as old as I look." Brad could see that Mort was struggling to remember his name. "My body's rickety. You wouldn't know what I mean because you're young and healthy. One day you'll wake up and find it hard to even get out of bed. Jesus, listen to me. What am I, a prophet of doom?"

"I hear we've got some rain coming in at the end of this week."

"Oh?"

"Big storm out over the Pacific. Coming in fast and cold and wet."

"Let's hope so. This goddamn drought has had us by the balls long enough. Be nice to see some green sprout up on my lawn again." Mort limped his way down the driveway. He stopped abruptly and looked in Brad's direction, as though he'd just remembered something. "By the way, if my cat comes around, don't feed him. He's a big black panther. Thinks he owns the block. Maybe he does. Don't feed him, cause he's mine."

BRAD WALKED UP Mort's driveway, cradling Mort's cat in his arms. He might just lay the cat on the porch and go on to work. It was just a cat, after all. But maybe he owed it to his neighbor to fess up. Brad reached a finger toward the doorbell. Heavy cat—fifteen, maybe twenty pounds.

Mort opened the door and stood there in his ragged bathrobe. The hair on the sides of his scalp stuck out like sprung wires. His hands dropped to his sides. "Ah, shit," he said.

Brad took a step back.

"Shit," Mort repeated.

"I'm sorry, Mort. I never saw him. He must've been stretched out in the sun there on my driveway as I backed out. If it's any consolation, I don't think he knew what hit him."

"Consolation? Are you kidding me?" Mort put his hands together palm to palm, like praying hands. "What a way to start the fucking day." Mort rubbed his whiskers. "Bring him in."

The house looked dark and dingy inside. A musk wafted out. As Brad stepped inside, he imagined his team sitting down at the conference table, a travel box of Peet's coffee and a tray of bagels on the cart next to his ergonomic office chair. He must have half a dozen "where r u?" texts on his phone by now—the phone sitting on the passenger seat of his Subaru.

Mort led him down the hall and into the kitchen. "Put him down there."

He pointed to the table where the newspaper was spread out. Brad lay the cat across the open sports page. Mort leaned against the counter and folded his arms. "That cat was the only friend I had. Some sonuvabitch was feeding him."

"Maybe it was Carol," Brad said.

"Carol's allergic . . . she collects everything but animals. Her husband was my buddy. We were in Korea. Did I already tell you this? Two weeks after we got home, he was hit by a drunk driver and paralyzed from the waist down. They used to call that irony."

"What do they call it now?"

"Huh?"

"You said they *used* to call that irony."

"I did? I don't know what I'm saying anymore." Mort pulled a mug down from the rack next to the Mister Coffee. He poured a steaming cup and placed it on the kitchen table next to the cat. He pulled out a chair and motioned for Brad to sit. "What have you got to say for yourself?" he asked.

"I'm really, really sorry, Mort."

"If I were ten years younger, I would punch you in the face."

"Let me buy you a new cat."

"Oh, hell, I don't want a new cat. I only took this one as a favor to somebody who was moving into a retirement home. The people who run those places are all twelve years old. They don't give a shit about old people."

"Let me do something to make it up to you," Brad said.

"Look—" Mort scratched his belly—"what's your name?"

"Brad."

"Look, Brad. I'm mad, but I know you didn't mean to kill my cat. Shit like this happens every day to somebody. Today I'm somebody."

The coffee was stronger than Brad was used to, but it was rich, with a nutty aftertaste. Brad looked out Mort's sliding glass door at his backyard, overgrown with shrubbery that had once made a neat row along the redwood fence. "You've got more yard space than I do," Brad said.

"Corner lot. Tremendous advantage on a block like this. Think about it. You've only got neighbor noise on one side. And my lot has three feet more space on the street side. I used to keep fish ponds over there. One very good year I had three dozen koi. It was a passion with me at one time, raising koi. This was when my wife was alive. She was Korean. They keep those fish as pets all over the Orient. They're surprisingly friendly for fish. Come right up to the surface and suck your fingers. Let you pet them all down their back."

"Koi." Brad nodded.

"Beautiful fish. No two exactly alike. What do you do for fun, Brad? You play any poker?"

"Not very well. I played in college, but ..."

"Bowl?"

"When I was a kid."

"Well, what are you good at?"

"Work, I guess."

"Do you live to work or work to live?"

"Pardon?"

"There are two kinds of people in this valley. Those who live to work and those who work to live. Which one are you?"

"Live to work, I guess."

Mort gestured with his mug of coffee. "When we were in Korea, Carol's husband and I, we had duty every night out along the perimeter at Outpost Harry. The Chinese lobbed their garbage at us. That's how close we were. We would lay in our foxhole and get pelted with kitchen waste from the Chink mess tent. And we'd lay there and dream of better days. We didn't expect to come home, you see. But we thought we might get to Tokyo. The Army was forever promising furloughs in Tokyo. We hoped we'd get laid by a geisha before we took a bayonet in the gut. Most of the guys in our unit went home in bags." Mort drained his coffee. "Hey, why don't you help me bury this beast?"

Brad shook his head. "There's a team of geeks sitting around a big conference table expecting me to show up and introduce our next project."

"Right. Carol's got my shovel anyway. Even if I knew exactly where it was, I don't think I could make it bite into this clay soil back here. I got no strength left." He slid open the big glass door. "Wait just one minute." He reached underneath his kitchen sink and pulled out a paper grocery bag. He held up one finger to Brad as he carried it outside to the corner of the yard and a grapefruit tree loaded with fruit. He picked several of the biggest grapefruit, dropping them in the bag. Mort shuffled back to the kitchen. "I can't eat these anymore. They react with my cholesterol meds. You may as well take some."

"Thanks."

"Maybe your geeks would like some fresh fruit. I've also got plums that'll come ripe in another two weeks. When they do, I'll make you up a box of them. I can't eat them. They give me diarrhea. By the way, what kind of project are you working on?"

"It's a new software program for the banking industry."

"Fucking banks. Things were much better when you could walk into a bank and talk to an actual person. In those days the tellers spoke

English and they would stamp your passbook and talk baseball. I hardly ever go inside anymore because when I do they act like I'm going to rob the place. It's all about the computers now, isn't it? Tell me something, do you think computers have souls?"

"I guess that depends on your definition of the word."

"The divine spark, that's what Carol calls it." He slid the glass door shut behind him and walked Brad to the front door. "Carol says the soul longs for union with God. And when we die, our soul joins all the other souls."

"I'm more concerned with what happens here and now," Brad said.

"When Carol's husband died, I was there with him. When the beeper on his life support flat-lined, I saw a change come over him, from a man with a personality and a sense of humor and an appetite, to a shell. An empty shell. His soul departed, you see, when his heart stopped, and I had the feeling that he was free of the prison that his body had become for him. I'm not saying it was a happy moment. But maybe it was a holy moment."

Brad stood awkwardly on Mort's front porch. Mort tightened the belt on his old bathrobe. "What do you think happens when we die?"

"When we die … the organism shuts down. Whatever we were, whatever dreams and aspirations we may have had, those just fizzle out, I guess."

"Well, aren't you a barrel full of laughs?" Mort said. His face broke into a wide grin. He began to chuckle. "You must be a hoot at a party!"

BRAD STOOD NEXT to his car and looked at the blood splotch on the driveway. He would need to uncoil the garden hose and wash that into the grass. His car was still idling. His cell phone was still sitting on the passenger seat. He carried the bag of grapefruit into the garage.

He drove the car back inside and turned off the engine. He picked up his cell phone and answered one of his team-members' texts: "resched meeting 4 2morrow. funeral to attend. L8R, brad." He tossed the phone back onto the seat.

He grabbed his shovel and closed the garage door. As he walked back to Mort's house, he balanced the shovel on his shoulder, like a rifle, and he rolled up his sleeves. How much trouble could it be, to bury a cat? Clay soil or no clay soil, he would only need to dig three feet or so, about the depth of a foxhole. And maybe afterward, he and Mort could do something about all that junk in Carol's side yard.

CRAWLSPACE

———❈———

H
E IS FLOATING IN SPACE, WEIGHTLESS, THE CAPSULE GENTLY
spinning like the beach boardwalk Tilt-A-Whirl. He feels giddy and lightheaded, then slightly nauseous. He half awakens to the sensation of peeing his pants. He feels warmth; he feels relief. The dizziness and the nausea subside as he awakens more fully. His conscious mind realizes he is peeing, and he makes the decision to just let it go. His joints ache. His legs cramp. His knees are tucked up under his chin. He is curled into the fetal position, arms wrapped around his legs. He smells the strong acrid odor of his own urine. As he opens his eyes, his thoughts return fully to the present. He is not in a space capsule; he is folded into a crawlspace beneath a mobile home in Sunnyvale, California, on the warm summer evening of his death.

Crickets chirp on the other side of the thin aluminum cover. The light coming in through the cracks is not as bright as it was in the afternoon when he had scurried up the side of the trailer to the carport, pulled the cover away and tucked himself inside. In the damp darkness, exhaustion set in. He gave himself over to it and drifted off. How long ago now had that been—three, maybe four hours?

He slips his hand inside his sweatshirt pocket and takes hold of the empty Glock. He had fired the first two rounds into the security booth at the entrance, sending Gerry, the gatekeeper, diving for cover. Had he hit Gerry? Blam. Blam. Then he had crossed the parking lot without incident. The responsible parties were all in the conference room, discussing him. They had placed him on suspension for "safety violations." *It's just routine,* Howie had told him to his face. *I gotta do this but don't take it personal. They want you to retrain on some of the machinery. Not my idea, you understand. Once you retrain and sign off on the safety procedures, then you can come back. Don't take it personal.* But he had overheard Howie tell Cameron that he would not be back. He would never be allowed back on site again. *Sayonara* fella. *Auf Wiedersehen* and *Adios.* That's all she wrote. *Toodaloo.* Goodbye and good luck.

He had fired two more rounds into Cheryl's reception desk. Blam. Blam. She blanched and raised her hands. She shook like she had the chills. *They're in the conference room, aren't they?* he had said, not asking, telling. *Don't,* she had said. *Please don't, don't, don't.* He fired again. Blam. Only ten left. Don't waste ammo. His thoughts were clear. His vision was sharp. He felt cool as a cucumber. They were meeting about his case, he knew. After eight years of such meetings, he knew exactly where each person sat, exactly what kind of donut each person ate, exactly how many bites each had taken by now, how much coffee had been drunk, and how many stupid jokes Scott had told about his fat wife and his fat brother-in-law.

He knew exactly how many steps it was from Cheryl's desk to the conference room: thirty-nine. Same amount of steps as in the old radio mystery he had read in junior high English class. Thirty-nine steps. Ten rounds more. Two shots each. He would fire two shots into each of them. One, two. One, two. And so on around the room.

Above him now, inside the mobile home, he hears footsteps and voices. A toilet flushes. A sink turns on, then off. A man's voice calls out. A woman's voice answers. In his mind's eye flashes his mother showing Gaby where to place her fingers on the piano keys. As Gaby plunked out the notes to the old hymn, his mother sang, *Great is thy faithfulness, O God my Father, there is no shadow of turning with thee.* The smile on Gaby's face as she accompanied her grandma. The throaty vibrato of his mother's voice. The warm light of their faces.

The clarity of the memory frightens him. He has not been frightened by anything all day. In fact, he has not felt any emotions at all. From start to finish, he had been mechanical and efficient and calm. *Thou changest not,* she sang, *thy compassions they fail not; as thou hast been thou forever will be.*

Deacon Andrew had said to him, *Man, you can't let this eat you up. You got to release this anger, brother. You talking crazy. Your mama called me in tears. She's worried what you might do. Your mind's caught in a loop of resentment. These people have wronged you, no doubt about that, but you got to let it go. You got to listen to the angels of your better nature.*

Angels and astronauts. He had watched the re-entry of the Apollo 13 capsule seated on his mother's lap. They crashed through the stratosphere with a fiery passion, then drifted and floated through the blue air above the Pacific, dangling from huge parachutes. *Thank you, Jesus!* his mother had cried. They floated there forever, it seemed, the capsule carried in the arms of invisible angels. At splashdown, his mother rose spontaneously to her feet and cheered. He had stood next to her, as amazed at her joyful outburst as he was over the miracle of three men who had been to the moon and back. Three men who now floated precariously in the middle of the ocean, jouncing and rocking in the huge waves, waiting for their large tin can to be pried open by the Navy Seals.

The moist earth beneath him smells rich and loamy. He is dripping with sweat. His nostrils are filled with his own ripe odor. Whatever liquid he has consumed in the past two days has seeped through his pores and peed into his jeans since entering the crawlspace. He feels completely dry and empty inside. Maybe there is a hose out there in the carport. He would like to hold the cold water up to his lips and fill his belly, then splash it over his head and face. Maybe strip off this sweatshirt and squirt himself down the way his mother had on certain summer evenings when, as a boy, he had come back from playing in the vacant lot. *Don't you bring that filth into my house, young man. Stand right there while I hose you down like a prize hog. Stand still now. Turn now, go ahead, turn around so's I can get your back.*

He sees now, in his mind's eye, the conference room as he came through the door. There they all were, seated around the table as he predicted. The coffee, the donuts, the manila folders, the mug full of sharpened pencils, the colored map of the cement plant on the wall next to the window, the sorry-ass bouquet of flowers that Cheryl had placed in the center of the big conference table. As if that could help. As if you could dress up that toxic dump with a few flowers.

He had pointed the gun first at Cameron, who stood as he spotted the Glock. Blam. Blam. The rest began to scatter. Julie screamed. He aimed at Howie next. Two-faced Howie. Howie who had trained him. Howie who had prayed for Gaby when Gaby fell from the top of the play structure and been taken by ambulance to the hospital. Howie who had driven him to the hospital and waited with him until the x-rays showed no broken bones. Howie who said to his face *don't worry about this* and then behind his back *so long sucker.* Blam. Blam.

Had he really gone through with it?

Outside the crawlspace he hears footsteps and whispers. He hears a scuffling of boots. And he thinks he hears a muffled voice over a sputtering radio device. He distinctly hears the word *perimeter*. The faint light coming in through the cracks around the crawlspace lid goes dark, then light again. Somebody has passed by, blocking the moon or the streetlight or whatever. He hears the phrase *roger that*.

He hadn't made a plan of escape. He hadn't expected to live. He'd felt certain that he'd be killed somewhere at the plant by one of the blue shirts who patrolled the place. He had not considered that he would be allowed to simply walk away as he had. To simply walk through the streets of the town. To enter the 7-11 and take a Gatorade and guzzle it right there in front of the cashier and walk out without paying. Probably he had been photographed on the surveillance cameras. The world was lousy with surveillance cameras. They would no doubt show him guzzling that Gatorade on the news tonight.

Julie had screamed and held up her hands and closed her eyes. She was weeping. *No, no, no.* Blam. Blam. Scott dove under the conference table and begged. *Think of my family*, he had said. *I've got kids, you idiot. I've got a family.* As if he didn't. As if only Scott mattered. Scott who had given him his initial tour of the plant. Scott who had called up his own landlord to give him a reference. He stooped and aimed the Glock. Scott scurried about, trying to hide behind the legs of the chairs. *My little boy just turned two. Oh, Christ, please. For God's sake. Please.* Blam. *Please.* Blam. The Glock felt warm in his hand. His fingers had molded to its shape.

Cool as a cucumber. His legs moved but he couldn't feel them. He walked out of the building. Squinted at the bright sunlight. And there was Bob the blue shirt running towards him. He raised the Glock. Bob dove behind his truck. The blue letters on the side of the white truck: Security. Blam. Blam. He kept walking. The gate stood open. There were people there. More blue shirts. They stood there on the perimeter of his vision, which was sharper than ever. All of his senses were alert. He had never experienced such clarity. The precision of moments. The sharp edges on everything: buildings, cars, trees. Familiar all of them. And new. He was seeing the world for the first time. It was all new. He walked. He stuffed the Glock deep into the pocket of his sweatshirt. He walked.

Just beyond the thin aluminum cover to the crawlspace he hears a snuffling—a police dog. Overhead, a helicopter. Chopity chopity chopity.

Gaby. What will become of her? What will they tell her about him?

Gaby, Gaby. It's time. He wants to stand up. He wants to stretch his legs. If he stands in the open and pulls out the Glock, they'll play their part. His body will twist and jerk from the impact. He will drop to his knees. Father, forgive us. He will fall and he will keep falling—through time and through space. He might drift there a while, carried by invisible angels. Who among the dead will greet him—his wife, his father, his brother?

Gaby, Gaby, Gaby. *Great is thy faithfulness! Great is thy faithfulness! Morning by morning new mercies I see.* He was holding Gaby's small hand in his. They were walking through the Smithsonian with his mother. And there it was, hanging from the skylight on thin wires: the Apollo 13 capsule. So small, he thought. So delicate. That thin, thin shell the only protection. You could punch through it.

He sees Gaby coming through the front door. It's afternoon. Warm light shines over her shoulder. She drops her backpack next to the sofa. An inaudible voice says to her, *How was your day?* She looks toward the voice. Her expression says joy. Her eyes say peace. Her smile says love. Her face shines, glows, fades, sunlight all around her head. She holds out her arms. She reaches to embrace him. Her face becomes pure light.

LEAF, FLOWER, BOLL

ON A HOT JULY AFTERNOON, I SLIP INTO THE AIR-CONDITIONED classic movie theater. The orchestra seats are packed, but up in the balcony there are only a few others besides me, and we are spread out, each in his own little zone of popcorn and soda and Good & Plenty.

The movie is a depression-era drama, set on a dilapidated farm in the Deep South. A widowed sister has come to live with her brother and his wife, who are struggling to bring the cotton in on time. In the opening scene, as the sister steps off the train, clutching her carpet-bag, a hailstorm sweeps through, damaging the crops and prompting the locals to wonder aloud if the sister has perhaps cast some sort of curse upon their little town.

The sultry heat that follows the hail makes it impossible to work through the afternoon hours. The husband rises well before dawn and works hard through the morning. His wife and sister shoulder all the house and barn chores. It's an impossible life, but life nevertheless. To top it off, the locusts are coming—a plague-sized brood sweeping down from the north.

There resides an unspoken tension between the sister and her brother, but the nature of the problem is never made clear. The brother has made room for the sister in his home but not in his heart. The wife makes subtle attempts at diplomacy, but neither the sister nor the brother seems interested in airing the problem, much less working toward a resolution. They labor in stoical silence.

I drift off to sleep, chin on chest. The movie becomes my dream. With the locust cloud on the distant horizon, the sister lugs an ax from barn to house. She goes inside. The dream camera never enters the house. It is fixed, for the moment, on a long tripod shot with the house on the left and the barn on the right. The large, dusty expanse between the buildings fills most of the frame, with that ominous cloud of insects occupying a gradually darkening piece of the sky.

After a long silence, noises can be heard from within, but they are indistinct, no more significant than those coming from the barn . . . horses shuffling, pigs snorting (or is that me snoring?), a muffled cry, a sudden rooster. Here and there a small twister of dust picks up and settles down.

The musical soundtrack is a moody, roots-style slide guitar and mouth harp—not at all the traditional orchestral score of the actual movie. It suits the grainy cinematography of my dream. The camera is stationary. The long silences and the small changes that gradually fill the frame are totally engrossing. Every element of the composition— the sinewy house and barn; the dusty, yawning expanse of the cotton field; the darkening sky—speaks with a spare elegance. Of what does it speak? Poverty of spirit. The husk of dignity upheld under enormous pressure. Perseverance tinged with despair. A looming sense of menace that underlies the mundane action. An artful plot of yearning or revenge, or both.

The sister emerges from the kitchen door with blood on the ax and a few buttons missing from her gingham dress. The screen door bangs shut behind her. She leans against the house and gazes vaguely over at the barn. She tucks a stray piece of hair back behind her ear. For a moment, it looks as though she might melt into the weathered siding, as certain lizards take on the camouflage of their rocky habitats. She absently leans the blood-stained ax against the house. Then she crosses the lonely space between house and barn, disappearing into its shadowy interior. Once again the camera lingers in the hazy light, the interior left to the viewer's imagination.

It is time for me to enter my own dream and play my part. I see myself enter the frame in worn slacks and work boots, a flannel shirt with the sleeves turned up. I wear a felt hat that needs to be cleaned and re-blocked. I come into the frame as if from the road and saunter up to the kitchen door, brushing dust from my shirt and wiping my forehead with a bandanna. I play the drifter, a familiar enough character in that period, an itinerant farmhand who has wandered onto the property looking for work, or so it appears.

A psycho-cinematic quilt, the dream movie sews together swatches from a few different genres—the Dust Bowl tragedy, the western, the family melodrama (with a touch of film noir), and maybe even the erotic crime spree romance. These familiar elements coalesce and somehow fit, but they leave the narrative direction open-ended. Is this a dream about a woman who snaps under the stress of hard work and extreme conditions, or is it a dream about a ruthless killer who stalks her prey then takes them unaware, or is it a dream of misguided greed fueled by desperate times?

Although the camera briefly favors me with a close-up, the brim of my hat casts a shadow over my eyes. I don't notice the ax. It's just a farm implement, after all. I knock on the edge of the screen door. I scan the scene, taking it all in as the camera, now from my perspective, from the drifter's POV, pans around to the house, the barn, the expanse. I notice the dark cloud looming in the distance but register no alarm, even though the soundtrack has picked up a low hum.

I cup my hands around my face and peer into the kitchen. I take off my hat and reach for the door handle. At that moment, a few chickens emerge clucking from the barn ahead of the sister as she steps out from the shadows and into the hazy sunshine. She wipes her forehead with the back of her hand. It's you, finally you, her face seems to say, as she recognizes me. She picks up the hem of her dress; her steps quicken. She has been anticipating my arrival. We have known each other, known and loved each other, loved and murdered together, murdered the sister's husband. She crosses the expanse with reckless urgency.

We kiss and whisper in the ecstatic tones of those who have sacrificed all to be together. Finally, the sister takes the hand of the drifter, my hand, and leads me into the house. The camera remains outside and records the stillness of the afternoon. The guitar and the mouth harp explore low tones in a minor key. The farm animals maintain their restless noisemaking in the background. They sense something, as animals often do.

The only thing moving within the frame is the rapidly increasing size of the insect cloud as the sky slowly drains of color. The gradual looming becomes a sudden engulfment. It becomes clear that the locusts have descended upon the cotton field. The music gives way to the deafening sound of the ravenous insects. In no time they strip each stem of leaf, flower, and boll—down to the fibrous roots.

The drifter and the sister emerge from the house. They turn to face the darkness. She takes up the ax once again and swings wildly at the onslaught. She weakens as she realizes her futility. The drifter takes the ax from her and leans it back against the house. Their clothing is ruffled as if by a great wind. Their mouths are agape and their faces writhe. The drifter pulls her to him in a final embrace, turns her body to the house. He covers her body with his, attempting to protect her from the swarm. The frame is consumed by the dark, swirling mass. Time slows. It seems this darkness and din will never pass.

Slowly, the cloud thins. The din recedes. The frame empties of chaos. The music can be heard once again: the low, slippery vibrato of the guitar, the moaning of the mouth harp. We see the silhouette of the lovers in their final embrace. No, it is only their skeletons we see, balanced tenuously against the siding, stripped of skin and muscle and blood and organs. The landscape has been purged utterly.

I awaken to the credits as they crawl up the screen. I am back. The orchestral violins of the actual movie soundtrack have awakened me. For a moment my mind is still full of desperation and loss—a doomed conspiracy of one murder to get free, another to gain a household. The sister and the drifter lost in the end, but lost together in the manner of romantic tragedy—in a lover's embrace.

I sit up straight. My throat is parched. I sip at my soda and savor the burning sweetness. I taste the salty dregs of my popcorn. There is another feature after the intermission. An inept fool will spend the night in a haunted house on a bet. He will uncover a gang of thieves by accident. He will bungle things hilariously and win the love of a pretty girl in the end. I've got half a box of Good & Plenty in my pocket. I am happy to be alive. Happy to sit in the air-conditioned sanctuary of the classic movie theater on a hot July afternoon.

Moss Beach

WALKING ALONG, JENNIFER WATCHES HER BARE FEET AS
they sink into the warm moist sand. She listens to the ripple of
the small waves and the shriek of gulls overhead. In the distance, a row
of pelicans skims the surface of the water. A steady breeze blows in from
the northwest. She wears a thin, summery cotton paisley skirt and a
navy tank top. She has twisted her hair into pigtails, the way her mother
taught her thirty years ago.

Up ahead a sailboat lies on its side, a recent wreck. She can see that
the hull has been battered and split upon the rocky reefs just offshore.
The boat has nothing to do with her, she tells herself. It is an object hewn
of wood and fiberglass and metal. Its crooked mast holds a ripped sail,
which flaps and flutters in the afternoon breeze. She is just a creature
upon a beach, with breath in her lungs and a slight hunger in her belly, a
bipedal organism walking in sand. And it is just a boat, not a metaphor
for her life.

A man is salvaging what he can from the wreck. He has taken the
seat cushions and stacked them on the rocks near the dunes. Now he
is trying to fold the tattered jib for transport, but the breeze is fighting
his efforts.

She stops to notice the gashes on the vessel's underside. The keel
has two big nicks in it. Someone long ago painted the name *Dana* on
the bow, just above the waterline on the right side of the hull, the side
now turned toward the sky. She walks around the boat. Across the stern
it says *Alameda*. It had sailed out through the Golden Gate two days
earlier and turned south against the powerful Farallon currents. Made
for pleasure cruising on the bay, this kind of sloop isn't really equipped

for the open sea. It is only a twenty-footer, and the sailor must have struggled mightily against current and wind. She notices the tiller has snapped and splintered.

One word might explain the sloop's presence on the sand: fog. Sometimes it moves in so fast you can't do anything but drop anchor, send out a locator ping, and hunker down until it moves on. This sailor may have been overconfident, or drunk, or just plain incompetent. But now she has stopped noticing and begun analyzing again, just as Father Banning warned. *Notice the movement of your thoughts*, he had instructed. *Don't judge them, and for God's sake don't give them suckle.*

She redirects her gaze toward the horizon. *Just this and nothing more*, she softly chants. Strips of wispy clouds hang just above the horizon. The breeze ripples her skirt. She feels the weight of her sandals in her left hand and the slight pull of the wind on the brim of the floppy hat in her right hand. *Just this.* The cold water suddenly surrounds her ankles. Her muscles tighten and her skin tingles. *Only this.* She focuses on her breath as she draws in the briny air. *This.*

JENNIFER AND LUIS lay on top of the sheets. The window was open and a breeze cooled them. In afterglow, the flush of freshly-oxygenated blood made their sweaty skin tingle; their breathing began to even out. Horns honked out on 18th Street, three floors beneath them. The screen on Jennifer's phone lit up. She looked to see who was calling. "I need to take this," she said to Luis.

Luis sat up and wiped his face with the edge of the sheet. He reached for a water bottle on the nightstand.

Jennifer said into her phone, "Hi, Jamie. What's up? Are you guys back home already?" Her son, Jamie, and her husband, Kenneth, had gone for a bike ride in the Presidio this morning, and Jennifer had taken the opportunity to meet Luis for a quickie in his Potrero Hill apartment.

The voice on the phone said, "This is Officer Shawn Casper of SFPD. I'm calling from Jamie Miller's phone. I dialed the contact labeled 'mom.' Is this Jamie's mom?"

"Yes."

"May I ask your name, please?"

"Jennifer Miller."

"Mrs. Miller, I just put your son into an ambulance on Lincoln Boulevard. He's currently in transit to SF General Trauma Center."

Jennifer couldn't speak.

"Ma'am? Hello? Mrs. Miller?"

"Yes."

"You need to proceed to the SF General Trauma Center immediately. Do you know where that is?"

"Yes."

"Is there someone there who can drive you?"

"Yes. Wait. Where's my husband? They were together. Let me talk to my husband. Wait. What happened? Has there been an accident? Put my husband on the line."

Jennifer heard the officer cover the phone with his hand. He muttered a garbled phrase that sounded vaguely like a question. She pictured him on the side of a road somewhere, possibly with a partner at his side. Two cops out on Lincoln Boulevard. She heard a receding siren in the background.

"Ma'am." He came back on the line. "There's another victim here. A middle-aged male with red hair in green and yellow bicycle attire."

"That's him. That's my husband, Kenneth. Is he all right?"

"He'll be transported to the same location. You'll want to arrive as soon as is safely possible. My partner and I will meet you there."

"Yes. I'm on my way."

Luis was standing next to the bed. Jennifer dropped her phone.

"You're white as the sheets," he said.

"Take me to SF General," she said, struggling to dress.

Luis pulled on his clothing and helped Jennifer with hers. He gathered up her phone and her earrings, her purse and her shoes. They hurried for the stairs.

JENNIFER HEARS A SERIES of barks. Farther up the beach a dog bounds into the water after a tennis ball, splashing and swimming out to it. The ball is lifted in a wave momentarily and then lost on the other side of its crest. The dog paddles on. The next wave brings the ball nearer. The dog takes the ball in its teeth and turns for shore, where its master claps and waits. Another creature among creatures. Notice the joy, she thinks, the unbridled joy of two animals, a dog and a man, playing a simple game in the surf. Pulling the tennis ball from the dog's jaws, the master praises his dog, who barks and barks at his feet. The man rears his arm back and launches it again into the waves. Into the waves again the dog splashes and bounds and gleefully swims.

JENNIFER MADE AN EFFORT to listen, but a few times she found herself staring politely at the other participants in the group as their mouths moved and their larynxes vibrated, as the air filled with the brittle noise of their grief. One by one they unburdened themselves with stories of loss and emptiness and confusion. Why had God robbed them of their joy? Would they ever feel normal again? Would they ever be loved again?

When her turn came, Jennifer spoke of her hours in the hospital following the phone call. She had been greeted in the ER by a Chaplain who escorted her to the treatment room where they had struggled to revive her son, and then to the morgue where they had taken the mangled body of her husband. All the while her phone filled with the text messages of her lover, Luis, who had circled the hospital twice after dropping her at the ER entrance and then driven to Land's End where he walked off the stress along the path all the way to China Beach.

She went ahead and gave voice to her worst fear: that her infidelity had somehow caused the accident. It was a cruel and illogical notion, she knew, but nevertheless there it sat, always perched on the edge of her thoughts. Was this what was meant by karma? Had her infidelity resulted in the taking of her family? Was this God saying, *If you can't handle a family, I'll just take it away*?

When everyone in the group had shared, Father Banning spoke of the need to forgive oneself. At this, Jennifer openly guffawed, covering her mouth and attempting to stifle the sharp, derisive laughter that sprang from her lips. She did not wish to disrespect Father Banning. She needed this group. Save this one uncontrollable outburst, she had suppressed her doubts. But this sprang from her lips before she knew it. She covered her mouth with one hand and raised the other in apologetic surrender. The group refocused its attention on Father Banning as he closed the session by once again leading them in the serenity prayer. *Fucking serenity prayer*, thought Jennifer. *Serenity my ass.*

AS JENNIFER ROUNDS the edge of the cliff, she finds herself among tide pools. She slips her sandals back on and chooses her steps with care, avoiding the slippery green seaweed. Waves splash over the rocks at intervals, filling the pools with swirling whitewater, temporarily obscuring the rocks altogether. As the water clears in the receding tide, she is able to peer in. She sees golden starfish, big purple urchins, clusters of mussels, and scuttling hermit crabs that migrate between crevices. Each pool is a world unto itself, isolated and discrete, but sharing the same nourishment from the tide's constant and universal motion. She squats low to see some anemones and fan-shaped limpets. A wave splashes into the pool, shocking her with its icy chill. She stands and feels her entire body tingle. *This, just this*, she thinks. *Only this*.

She gazes up at the tall cypress trees jutting from the top of the cliff, a few clinging precariously to the sandstone, held in place by deep and resilient roots. Some of the trunks are bare. Some are heavy with branches loaded with green needles. Some of the needles are crusted with a rust-colored fungus prompted by the brine. The trees are slowly marching into the sea, and the sea is slowly advancing upon the shore, pulling the cypress trees in—a geological dance along the rim of two tectonic plates. It is a place of beauty and violence, new life and slow death.

A lone heron stands on the farthest edge of the tide pools, gazing out to the horizon. Is it awaiting a mate, or keeping an eye out for prey? No, she will not speculate. She squelches her projections and turns her mind once again outward. She sees the iron pillar a quarter mile out, beyond the waves. The first time she saw it she thought it was a sculpture of a human figure, perhaps a tribute to the surfers or the fishermen or the lighthouse keepers. But with a pair of opera glasses one day she was able to focus on its rough-hewn metallic shape, covered with mottled mollusks. A sign back on the dunes explained it had been placed there by the US Navy during WWII and used for target practice. Destroyers and submarines had calibrated their weapons at this spot before setting out across the Pacific.

JENNIFER WAS WANDERING again. She had left home at midday, stopped at a familiar strip mall for a taco and a soda, and walked in a new direction, along strange residential streets, looking at the houses and the cars and the shabby parks and aging schools. She had come to another strip mall, this one too high-end for a taco shack. These were boutique clothing shops and jewelry stores and gift emporiums stuffed with beach-themed tchotchkes and knick-knacks. Down at the end of the strip, she saw a coffee shop. She was thirsty. Very thirsty. She had walked and walked.

Halfway down the row, she stopped at the window of an art supply store. They were having a sale. Jennifer had always wanted to paint, but she had never taken the time to try it. Oh, she had had the odd art lesson in school—fingerpaints early on, then drawing lessons, primarily geometrical shapes, and later the color wheel, and some basic theory of line, perspective and composition. Nothing to inspire further interest. But she had always been captivated by the great paintings she had encountered in galleries and museums. Now she wanted to paint more than anything.

When the bell over the door rang out, she was greeted by a teenage girl with a major nose ring. "Hey," the girl said, "stupendous sale this week. Try to control your impulses. The best deals are around the edges of the store—canvases and brushes are half off, and if you're not picky about brands, some good quality oils and acrylics. Watercolor stuff goes on sale next month. Let me know if you need any help." The girl disappeared into the back of the store.

Jennifer picked up a how-to book on painting with acrylics. She forgot her thirst. As she flipped through the pages of sample student paintings, she realized she could do this. The yearning to paint, latent for years, had been a signal that had gone unheeded. Yes, she could do this. And what better way to help her follow Father Banning's mindfulness training? *Just this.* A blank canvas. *Only this.* A brush dipped in color. *This.* A swath of sky. Clouds. A shoreline. Gulls. A woman walking along a beach, her sandals in one hand, a floppy hat in the other.

JUST AROUND THE CORNER from the cliff, tucked back into a grove of cypress trees, sits a shingled cottage, the perfect ocean retreat. Jennifer imagines herself passing long days in the cottage, with a wood fire in the stove and fog curling about the house, a pot of tea steeping, her canvas locked into an easel before the big picture window, no one near, no one approaching, only the pounding of waves, perhaps Debussy on the stereo and, in the distance, a fog horn.

What would she paint? Perhaps the cottage itself in its idyllic little setting, a warm light glowing in the kitchen windows. She might feel the need to paint her memory of Luis, his dark, lithe body against the white sheets. She might eventually need to paint the mangled bicycles that her brother had retrieved from the police station storage facility. And she might also need to paint the doctor's delicate hands holding his glasses when he explained that her husband and her son had been killed by a drunk driver in broad daylight on a dry, sunlit road next to the most beautiful bay in the world, within sight of the famous red-orange bridge. He had removed his glasses when he sat next to her in the waiting room and held them in his lap, loosely gripped between the thumb and forefinger of his left hand.

Pinned to the lapel of the doctor's white coat was a photo button of a young girl in a numbered jersey. She held a soccer ball in her hands and stared from the photo with a confident, determined look. Instead of looking into the doctor's eyes as he spoke, Jennifer had stared at the photo of the girl, and then she let her gaze fall to those delicate hands in his lap, gripping the tortoise shell frames. She could not remember the doctor's face. Was his hair blond or brunette, salt and pepper, or totally gray? Her composition would focus on the glasses and the poised hand that held them. She thought she could paint the folds of his slacks as a background to the simple pair of glasses loosely held between thumb and forefinger.

There are some large rocks just ahead on the sand. No, she jumps back, startled. Not rocks. Harbor seals. Dozens of them. They have dragged themselves from the surf and positioned themselves along the beach like teenagers working on their tans. She walks around them, giving them plenty of room, but watching, noticing. *Just this. This and nothing more.* Creatures on the beach. And she just another creature.

Suddenly she feels exhausted, as if she can no longer stand. She plops down in the sand between the cottage and the harbor seals. She lay back onto the warm sand, placing her sandals and her hat next to her. She closes her eyes and gives herself over to the warmth of the sun. She puts herself into the care of the waves and the barking dog, the screech of the gulls and the sound of children playing nearby in the surf. *This. Only this.* There will be no dreams in this nap. Just darkness. Only darkness. And rest. And then again light and energy. She will awaken to a slight chill in the air but the sun still bright in her eyes. And there will be breath in her lungs and a slight hunger in her belly, a real and genuine hunger. The light. The breath. The hunger. *Just this.*

All the Daughters of
Song Are Brought Low

M AMA AND I WALKED OUT TO THE EDGE OF THE WINDY CLIFF
with our new friend Reynaldo. He paced up and back along the
precipice, crushing the ice plant beneath his boots, before he sat on
the bench and drew the shape of Split Rock into a small sketch pad. It
was a cold day; the mist blew across the face of the cliff, obscuring then
revealing Straggler's Cove down below. As the tide slowly went out, the
gray sand looked slick as a seal's pelt.

"I love the sparkles in the wet sand," Mama said. "They shine like
stars."

"That's mica, otherwise known as fairy dust," Reynaldo said, winking
at me. He tucked his sketch pad into his rucksack and gathered up the
tools of his trade—two rakes: a large one with thick prongs that narrowed
into dangerous-looking spikes, and a smaller one with flexible prongs,
the kind you might use to gather dry leaves. "I'm off," he said. Holding
the rakes together like an acrobat with a balancing pole, Reynaldo
disappeared from our view and made his way down the cliffside.

A few minutes later he reappeared at the bottom—so small I thought
he looked like a Reynaldo doll. He took off his boots and walked barefoot
out across the sand. He began at the base of Split Rock and, using a rake
in each hand, worked his way outward, mimicking its shape with the
large rake, turning the sand dark as the prongs churned it, then tracing
those thick lines with the smaller rake, creating the illusion of a series of
nearly-identical islands, all in the shape of the big rock.

Mama and I sat on the bench eating cucumber sandwiches and

watching Reynaldo transform the beach into a giant canvas. Mama had met Reynaldo the night before, in Frank's Place where, she said, he had drunk three fishermen under the table and was yet sober enough to dance a slow dance with her and not crush her toes. Mama never danced with those fishermen because they knew Daddy, and because they stank of fish. Reynaldo was just passing through, smelled of Old Spice and, according to Mama, had the good sense to put Gordon Lightfoot on the Juke Box. They danced a slow whirl under dim lights.

The symmetrical pattern Reynaldo carved into the sand around Split Rock reminded me of the amoebas we had looked at under the microscope in biology lab that fall. The assignment was to look through the scope and then draw what we saw on sketch paper, labeling the nucleus and the ectoplasm and the pseudopodium. Mama pointed out that the shapes Reynaldo was making were all echoes of the shape of Split Rock, the craggy volcanic formation that looked like twin islands when the tide was in, but was revealed to be two humps of a single rock when the tide was out.

A tiny dancer, Reynaldo moved like a graceful ant in large, wavy circles, churning a geometrical pattern of dark shapes from the slick, wet sand. The beautiful design that gradually emerged for us he could not himself see but only imagine. His art was to carve the sand with the rakes, each an extension of an arm, all the while picturing our elevated viewpoint in his mind. In such a way he had created dozens of "sand paintings" up and down the west coast, each lasting only a matter of hours before being erased by the incoming tide. After photographing each design, he packed up his tools and drove on up the coast highway to the next town, the next cove, with his well-worn book of tide tables, his sketch pad, and his taste for Kentucky bourbon, not to mention the ballads of Gordon Lightfoot.

As he neared completion of his Straggler's Cove piece, our neighbors gathered along the cliff edge. Word had spread that something odd and wonderful was happening. Sure enough, and sure enough: the shaggy stranger who had out-drunk their friends and seduced my mother while my father was at sea was down in the cove, fool that he must be, deliberately making something that could not last.

When he appeared again at the top of the cliff, he did not bother to answer their questions. He snapped a few photos of the beach with his old camera. He gobbled our remaining cucumber sandwich and guzzled the beer mama had packed for him. We followed him to his pick up truck. In the bed of his truck he pulled back a canvas to reveal a suitcase that belonged to us. It had occupied a place on the top shelf of our broom closet as long as I had been alive. When Mama saw the look of confused recognition on my face, she took me by the shoulders and got her face down to the level of my face, her eyes looking into my eyes. "Don't hate me," she said.

Our new friend Reynaldo turned out not to be a friend, after all, but a thief, who stole Mama out from under my nose that early November day. One moment we were sharing sandwiches at Straggler's Cove and the next he and Mama were dropping me back at the house and driving away without me.

WHEN DADDY CAME through the kitchen door later that evening, he couldn't look me in the eye. He'd already heard the news down on the docks. Everything you needed to know in our little town could be learned as the fishermen unloaded their haul, packed their catch in ice, and loaded the crates onto the market and restaurant trucks. Over the cries of the gulls hovering above the boats, the news was passed. By the time those trucks filed through the village and made the southbound turn onto the coast highway toward San Francisco, everybody knew exactly what had happened while our small fleet was out.

We both stuck to our routines, Daddy and me: I sat at the little desk pretending to do homework as he washed out his thermos in the sink. Then he stripped to his skivvies, tossing the fishy clothing in the basket on the sand porch, and went to scrub the stink of the boat from his hair and skin. Mama had never let him kiss her until he'd had his shower. She meant business, too. I remember the resounding smack of her hand across Daddy's cheek the one time I saw him try.

I heard him banging drawers in the bedroom. He slammed the closet door. He was checking to see what all she'd taken. Sure enough, and sure enough: most of her clothing was gone, along with what jewelry she had. I heard the medicine cabinet squeak. No, she had left her sleeping pills behind. He shook the bottle. The toilet flushed. When I heard the water come on in the shower, I realized I'd been holding my breath.

The house was silent except for the sound of the shower. Usually Mama had music on in the evening. I went over to the hi-fi. What record should I put on? Daddy's favorite was a Pete Fountain album with lots of loopy-sounding horns. That didn't seem right. Mama would usually put on her Sandy Denny record while she cooked. That didn't seem right either. I decided on Elvis Presley Live in Las Vegas.

I heated up Daddy's favorite Campbell's soup—potato leek. Before sitting next to me, he opened a new pack of Saltines and got himself a beer from the cooler. We sat together like a pair of clean-smelling zombies, staring at mama's oil paintings, which hung on every wall of the house—pictures of the harbor, the boats, the cove at sunset, our cottage with the big magnolia in the yard, a self-portrait of Mama wrapped in one of Daddy's nylon fishing nets.

"Homework finished?" he asked.

"It's Friday," I said.

"Oh. Right," he said.

"But I did our weekend homework all already."

"Math, too?"

"Math, too."

"Time for your shows," he said, looking at his watch.

Daddy put our dishes in the sink as I plopped in front of the television and stared at *The Brady Bunch* and *The Partridge Family* and *Room 222* while daddy cleaned and organized his tackle out on the porch. During *The Odd Couple*, I made Daddy a cup of coffee the way he likes it, with two sugars, and brought it outside to him. His work finished, he was looking through the telescope. I flipped off the kitchen light and the porch light so he could better see the night sky.

"Look here," he said.

I covered my right eye and looked into the eyepiece.

"Saturn," he said. I saw his copy of *Burnham's Celestial Handbook* on the railing, and I knew he'd already checked it.

"She's a beauty," I said. "It's got a kind of a pinkish glow around the edges."

"You're looking across 700 million miles of space." He lit his pipe and sat on the porch swing to drink his coffee.

"What do we do now?" I asked.

"Enjoy the view," he replied. "It's not every night you can see Saturn."

"No, I mean . . . now what do we do?"

"We've both got plenty to do. I've got the boat. You've got school. We'll keep doing that." He puffed his pipe and blew the smoke up into the dark. "Would you like me to have Grandma come out and stay with us for awhile?"

I shook my head no. I didn't need any help. Mama was a drinker, so I'd been caring for myself and the house as long as I could remember.

Daddy was hurt and angry, but I think he always expected that someday she would leave. She didn't like the village, hated the smell of fish, and always thought of herself as an outsider, even, I know now, in her own home. More than once she had stood in front of the painting of her tangled in Daddy's fishing net and made the palms of her hands look like gills on the side of her neck. She was the only one who thought that was funny, and when she was drunk, she would laugh a raspy bitter sort of laugh, making a fishy mouth by opening and closing the iris of her lips like a cartoon goldfish.

WHEN MAMA WASN'T drinking she was thinking of drinking. Mornings she was groggy and slow. By noon she grew restless and itchy and irritable. Nothing could settle her. The long hours between noon and three were the witching hours—people in the village knew to steer clear of her then. There were enough dented fenders and bullied clerks and kicked dogs around town to testify to this.

It wasn't until her first drink of the day, sometime between three and five o'clock, that she settled. Once that first drink went down, the only one she really tasted, she could relax and think about stuff, and people besides herself, with clarity and efficiency. If I needed help with homework I would catch her on her second glass. Two drinks in and she was golden. Everything clicked for her then. She buzzed and hummed like a bee in clover. The first two were guzzled, but her third drink was usually sipped at the kitchen sink, looking out at the magnolia tree, swaying to Sandy Denny or Joni Mitchell or Joan Baez, songs of female lament. These women, too, had been caught in nets and knew the feeling.

The fourth drink was my cue to get out of her way, preferably out of the house—to the public library or the rec center or the harbor—and stay away until she grew drowsy. Drinks four and five, that was the danger zone, when she said and did the things she later regretted. With drinks four and five in her belly she was a chaos monster looking for someone, anyone, to devour. If Daddy was home, it was him. If she was out somewhere, it was a bartender or a traffic cop or, to Daddy's great embarrassment, the harbor master.

Once she got to the drowsy stage, about the sixth drink, she became weak and weepy and contrite. If I could get some coffee into her, she might play card games with me, or she would reminisce about her own life as a girl and all the places she'd seen as a Navy brat after the war—the Philippines and Okinawa and Alaska. But if I couldn't get her to take some coffee, she would sink into the sofa and stare at the TV until about midnight, when she would wander down to Frank's Place. If Daddy was home he would get her to take a walk after drink three and distract her with a movie, or he would set out her paints and easel and convince her to work.

The only time Mama found consolation was when she was absorbed in a painting. She would hum and sing to herself and talk her way through the creative process. Mixing her colors and carving out pictures in oil brought her true solace. Every line on her face smoothed out when she painted. The muscles in her jaw and her neck and shoulders relaxed. Her eyes, blue-gray as the ocean, shone with calm delight.

TWO DAYS LATER we each got a letter from Mama. We sat together at the kitchen table to read them. Daddy read slower than me, so I read mine twice to keep from finishing before him. Neither one of us cried then over what Mama wrote. I did plenty of crying alone. But I did not cry in front of Daddy. And he did not cry in front of me. We were brave soldiers, the two of us. I snuck into Daddy's top dresser drawer one day to read his letter. I could tell she had written both our letters after the sixth drink because there wasn't a mean or angry word in either one. She was sorry, she said. She knew what she had done was wrong. She hoped to make it up to us some day.

Daddy got one more letter from her in the spring, asking him to wire some money. I got a letter every two weeks or so for awhile, letters filled with the same apologies as the first and a few sentences each about where they were, her and Reynaldo, and how the weather was there, and about some of the people they met. I stopped opening them after awhile, and then they stopped coming.

We did fine, Daddy and me. The teachers at school were extra nice. The librarian asked if I needed help with my homework. The clerk at Smith & Son's started a tab for us so I could pick up a bag of groceries when I needed to. That way Daddy could go in on payday and just write him a check for what we owed. One of the neighbor ladies brought us a pie now and then, saying it wasn't any trouble at all to cook an extra one whenever she baked. She also said she was not one to judge but she guessed we were both better off this way. When a woman takes to the bottle like Mama, she said, there was no good that could come of it.

Often I would wake at 3 A.M. when Daddy did and help carry some of his equipment down to the boat with him in the dark. We practiced naming the constellations on those walks. Then I would sit out on the jetty and wait for the *Delilah* to chug past, and Daddy would wave from the little window in the pilot's house. I walked home and slept a little more before school.

Sometimes at night, when I closed my eyes, I saw Straggler's Cove with Reynaldo's design in the sand, the one he carved that day that he and Mama left. One day when Daddy took the boat down into the Alameda yards for maintenance work, I got Mama's paints out and set up her easel in the living room, right in front of the big window so the light was good. I laid out some colors on the palette the same way Mama did, and I painted that scene. I painted Mama and me sitting atop the cliff. I painted the tide out and Split Rock fully exposed. And I painted as best I could the shapes Reynaldo had made in the sand. But I did not paint Reynaldo—that would have been a betrayal of Daddy.

I hung the painting up in my bedroom so I could see it when I was lying in bed. Mornings I would look up at it. I suppose it was my way of preserving something that was never meant to last. In my picture, the tide would never wash the art away. Mama and I would forever sit there together, eating cucumber sandwiches, at that moment when the sand sparkled like the stars, and the foamy tide had not yet erased the beauty.

MAMA CAME HOME to us the next summer. For a few weeks it was the three of us again, back to our old way of being. She had written me a letter explaining that Reynaldo had dumped her and her suitcase at a train station up in Oregon with just enough cash to buy a ticket home. That was one of the letters that I stuffed unopened into the bottom of my underwear drawer at the time. I read all the letters eventually, but it would be awhile before I had the stomach to learn in her own words what had happened.

Mama pretended to be her old self, even making an effort to play games with me and take me for walks. But I could tell she was different. Daddy wasn't fooled for a minute. He could see that her drinking had worsened. And she couldn't pretend as she once had for my sake to like him or the boat or the town or her life with us. She was kind to me, but when she thought I wasn't listening, or was safely in the other room out of earshot, she lit into him, ridiculing his life and his manner and even his looks. Daddy just took it.

She started earlier in the day and accelerated her drinking routine in order to achieve and then maintain the numbness and the steady hum in her head. Her body had changed in the intervening months. Her face was puffy and her skin had grown splotchy and her eyes could not rest on any object or person for long. When she spoke to Daddy she closed her eyes completely as if she couldn't stand to look at him.

Then one night, after I'd gone to bed, I heard her screaming at him in the kitchen. The words came through the walls in brittle spurts, as if she were spitting them into his face. And for the first time I heard Daddy screaming back, standing up to her and giving back what he had taken for so long. I heard drawers opening and closing, cupboards slamming, furniture scooting. A lamp shattered against the living room wall right next to my closed bedroom door. I was frozen beneath my covers. The light of the moon shone through my window. I focused on my painting of Straggler's Cove, trying to tune out the noise, and I eventually drifted off.

I awoke sometime later to utter silence.

When I opened my bedroom door, mama was lying on the sofa staring up at the ceiling. She sat up and motioned for me to come sit next to her while she drained the bottle she'd been nursing. That was another thing that had changed: she no longer bothered to poor her booze into a glass.

Listen to this now, she said. She couldn't stop drinking, not for anyone, not even for me, her baby girl. Her father had drunk himself to death and she guessed she would do the same. She couldn't see any way out of it now, or any reason to try and avoid the inevitable.

Listen to me, she said, taking me by the shoulders, nothing in this world is made to last. Not one goddamn thing. The sooner I learned that the better. Try to hold on to something, she said, just try. You don't even need to take my word for it. Just keep your eyes open. You'll see for yourself. Your life will teach you. You don't even need a mother, she said. You're smart enough to figure this out by yourself. Just keep your eyes open.

Some people think *this* helps, she said, holding up the empty bottle. But it doesn't. It dulls the pain for a while, and then it doesn't. Some people think love helps, and it does for a while . . . until it doesn't. Does any of this make sense? she asked. Am I even speaking so that I can be understood?

She had taken a knife from the kitchen and slashed all of her paintings. The tattered strips of canvas hung limply from the edges of the frames. She had cut Daddy, too, though she hadn't meant to. He was trying to stop her from destroying her canvases, and she accidentally sliced into his arm. He had wrapped the wound in the dishtowel, she said, and driven himself to the hospital to get it stitched up.

She put on side two of her Sandy Denny album and sat with me on the sofa, softly singing the words and stroking my hair until we fell asleep together.

WHEN I AWOKE the next morning, she was gone for good.

Daddy sat at the kitchen table with his arm in a canvas sling. He had driven her to the bus station. She knew someone way down in Tijuana who would take her in, he explained. It was the best choice out of a slew of lousy options.

While I had slept on the sofa that morning, Daddy took down all of the ripped and sliced paintings from the walls and made a pile of them on the front porch. After dark that night he carried them with his one good arm down to the driveway and set them on fire. Sure enough, and sure enough: they made a beautiful show. The oil and the varnish burned with a hot, colorful fire, spitting sparks and thick smoke into the night sky, the wooden frames crackling and crumbling apart.

I went into my bedroom and took my own painting down off the wall. I tossed it onto the conflagration and watched it burn. We had our own little bonfire of the vanities right there under the magnolia, proving Mama right once and for all. None of it was made to last . . . not the oil paintings, not the sand carvings, not even our little family, such as it was. Not one goddamn thing.

Deeper Blue

C AM JOHNSON SAT ON THE CURB ACROSS THE STREET FROM the cop's house. He had been sitting there for half an hour, waiting. Although the curtains were drawn, the front window was open; Barry Manilow was on the stereo. Children's voices drifted through the window, too. They were playing. Whenever their game reached a climax, their voices rose to an excited pitch. In the tree out front, four crows kept watch. The sky overhead was pale blue, with the sort of low, wispy clouds that seemed to sit in the same place for hours.

The tan station wagon turned the corner. There he is, thought Cam. Son of a bitch. The wagon turned into the driveway. The horn honked. The front door opened, and the cop's wife stood there. She was a pretty woman with long red hair, in a sleeveless summer dress and sandals. She held a kitchen towel in one hand. The children squeezed past her and ran to greet their father.

As the cop pushed open the car door, the kids squealed and reached for him. He scooped the baby into his arms, a two-year-old girl, and he rubbed the short hair on his four-year-old son's head. The daughter had a pacifier in her mouth and her red hair up in a ponytail on the top of her head. The son was a miniature version of his father, with the same blond crew cut.

Cam kept his place on the curb and watched them unload their father's things from the car. The little girl clung to her father while he cradled her in one arm and gathered a stack of papers in the other. The boy carried his father's police hat and holster into the house. The cop's wife kissed him. They disappeared into the warmth of their home.

Cam had slept fitfully the night before. A movie of the whole thing played in his imagination. He kept seeing the cop pushing his friend down on the sofa and clamping his hand around her mouth as he pried her legs apart. Cam kept thinking about her broken retainer, the metal wire stabbing the inside of her cheek as he squeezed her face. Cam imagined the muffled cry and the futile attempts to push him off.

It had happened there, in the house right next door to the cop's. And right next door to that, on the corner, was his friend's house. She had known the cop all her life. In fact, he had helped the family when her mother had died suddenly of a brain aneurysm. The cop and his wife had been good neighbors to them in their shock and grief, organizing meals and transportation. That was why his friend let him into the house that night. The house right next door, where she was babysitting little Raymond.

Cam sat on the curb now and replayed his plans, such as they were. He would wait here on the curb until the cop arrived home. Then he would stand and cross the street, catching him by surprise as he got out of the station wagon. Cam had considered arming himself with a baseball bat. Maybe he would smash the windshield of the cop's car to get his attention. But the bat would not have allowed him the time needed to tell the cop who he was and why he was there. Anyway, the cop would have used his strength and martial arts training to disarm and disable him. Cam would have been quickly humiliated and silenced before he had the chance to confront the cop with his crime.

To do the righteous thing he would need a gun, and he would need to be prepared to use it. He would have to take the cop by surprise. If the cop saw him coming, he would simply use his own weapon in self-defense. No, the element of surprise would be crucial. He needed the cop to stand still and pay attention. It was the words, above all, that needed to be said—whatever may happen afterwards.

But Cam didn't have a bat or a gun. It occurred to him only now, as he sat impotently on the curb across the street from the cop's house, that he should have devised a way to get the cop's own gun and turn it on him. The poetic justice in that was sweet. Maybe sneak into his house, find the gun, and confront the bastard with his own civic-issued weapon. Now that was brilliant. But how could he possibly get the cop's gun? He would have it locked up somehow and hidden away. With children in the house, he would have some system for safety. Cam had not planned on the children. Had not imagined the *Father Knows Best* scene in the driveway.

The cop had come to the door that night after dark, after his friend had already put little Raymond to bed. She had been sitting on the sofa, watching television. She thought it strange that he should just appear at the front door. He asked if she was alone. That might have been a clue. He asked if little Raymond was asleep. It didn't occur to her until afterwards that he already knew the answers to these questions. And then when he said that big Raymond had asked him to look at the pipes under the kitchen sink, well, she didn't think that was strange at all, given his reputation as a good neighbor. Later, she told Cam, she soaked in a hot tub and washed and washed but still felt dirty.

As she described the rape to him, Cam felt a numbness growing within. The numbness wore off after a while, like Novocaine, leaving an ache. Then arose anger and fantasies of revenge: knocking on the cop's door and hitting him repeatedly with a baseball bat, knocking at the cop's door and firing bullets one after the other into his chest.

Cam sat on the curb across the street and remembered the fear in his friend's voice when she repeated for him the threat the cop made when he was finished: "Tell anyone and I'll get your sister next."

The curtains in the living room window parted. Then the cop opened his front door and came outside. The crows in the tree took flight. He looked up at the sky. He sauntered over to the edge of the lawn and turned on the sprinklers. He walked to the street, his feet on the edge of the curb, and looked up and down. The cop stepped into the street.

As Cam watched the cop approach, he realized that he was holding his breath. He had never had to tell himself to breathe before. The cop stood in front of him. Cam shielded his eyes as he looked up.

"How you doing, buddy?" the cop asked, a little too loud. "What's your name?"

Cam put his hands down at his side, gripping the edge of the curb.

"Nice afternoon, isn't it?" The cop took a step closer. The friendly tone in his voice disappeared. "Do we have a problem?" the cop asked.

Cam lowered his gaze to the cop's shoes.

"Young man, I asked you a direct question." The cop turned to look up the street. Two kids at the upper end of the block left their driveway on their Stingrays. He waved to them. "Why don't you stand up?"

Cam shifted his weight and lifted himself. He looked at the cop's face.

"You want to tell me why you're watching my house?"

Cam shrugged.

"Is there something you'd like to say to me?"

Cam shrugged again.

"If so, I'd like you to say it and then leave so I can go back inside and have dinner with my family."

Cam was standing in the gutter. The cop stood before him on the asphalt. The cop stepped even closer. Cam looked past him, over his shoulder, at the house the cop had entered on the night his friend was babysitting little Raymond. And then Cam looked at the next house, the one where his friend lived, just two houses down from the cop.

The cop turned his head to look in the direction Cam had looked. He smiled, turned back to Cam. He laid his forearms heavily on Cam's shoulders and leaned in. Leaned in as though they were buddies and as though he were confiding in Cam. The cop had beer on his breath. Beer and something else, something both sharp and sour. The cop spoke in a normal tone of voice, only inches from Cam's face so that Cam could not bring the cop's face into focus. Cam avoided the cop's eyes, which were staring down at him.

"When I go back into my house, something is going to happen. What's going to happen is this. You're going to walk away and never return. You're going to crawl back under the rock you crawled out of today. If I ever see you in front of my house again, I will do this to you. I will pinch your head off your scrawny neck and shove it so far up your ass you'll never find it again. Your mommy and your daddy won't be able to recognize you. They'll be left to wonder how big the mac truck was that ran over their baby boy." The cop removed his forearms from Cam's shoulders. He stood upright again. "I hope I've made myself clear."

The cop walked slowly away, glancing casually up and down the street as if he owned it. Owned it all—every house, every lawn, every tree, every garbage can and mailbox, every car and every bicycle. Without looking back at Cam, he turned off his sprinklers and went into his house, the front door clicking shut behind him.

Cam's knees gave way. He sank back down to the curb, landing hard on its edge. He scooted himself back a bit, back onto the cool grass of the parkway. He lay on the grass and looked at the sky. He put his hands at his sides to brace himself against the feeling that he was spinning. Only this grip on the grass and the soil beneath him would hold him in place. The sensation was like a carnival ride, the one where gravity pulls you and you fight against it at first, and then finally realize that the only solution is to give in to it.

A new emotion surfaced. Cam had at first felt disgusted by the cop, then angry, and then afraid. Now there was a hollowness within. A dry, empty pit in his stomach. The spinning sensation slowed. The sky overhead had darkened to a deeper blue. The sun lit the edges of the clouds, which were moving faster now. The crows announced their return to the branches of the cop's tree. So this is how it was, life in the world of adults. So this is how it would be.

ALL THE BIG JERKS
WHO RULE THE WORLD

Beverly Hilton Hotel, Los Angeles, 1979

CAM JOHNSON HAS HIS FINGER ON THE CALL BUTTON OF THE staff elevator and one of the hotel's skimpy pool towels wrapped around his shoulders. He's shivering. His hands and feet are pruned. The baggy swim trunks his supervisor loaned him hang limply down to his knees. He's dripping pool water onto the chartreuse carpet. He reeks of chlorine. All he wants is to get back down to the basement where he can change back into his street clothes, clock out, and squeeze in as much sleep as possible before the evening shift begins.

The bell rings; the elevator doors slide open. There, leaning against the wood paneling, is the great man himself, Juju Welch. He's wearing dark sunglasses, a pork pie hat, and a crumpled vest. His wild, curly, too-blond hair is pulled back into a ponytail. He looks like he's been up partying all night for about two hundred consecutive nights. Blotchy, unshaven, disheveled, he hasn't seen the sun in weeks. On stage, he looks like a Greek god; in person, he looks like something a cat coughed up, which just shows what good lighting and a little charisma can do. It helps that most of Welch's adoring fans are stoned out of their minds by showtime.

He's sipping from a coffee mug with the band's logo on it. When he looks up and sees Cam, he does a spit take, spraying dark liquid all down his front, laughing like his cartoon prototype Top Cat. "What the hell happened to you, kid? Somebody flush you down the toilet?"

"I've been fishing your goddamn television sets out of the swimming pool."

Cam has been diving to the bottom of the deep end of the hotel's pool all morning, retrieving the various plastic, glass, and metal pieces of the three RCA TV sets that actually hit water from Welch's sixth-floor window. Cam's co-workers, Jimmy and Juan Carlos, spent the morning cleaning up the shards of the sets that missed the pool and shattered onto the concrete patio, in one case nearly missing a room service cook who made the mistake of cutting across the pool deck on his way to the kitchen.

Welch pulls off his shades and props his bare foot against the elevator door, holding it open. "So you're the clean-up crew?"

"Me and about a dozen other people. We're working overtime because of you. The carpenters and wall board guys are waiting in the lobby for your party to check out so they can get in there and rebuild the rooms you trashed."

If his supervisor heard Cam saying these things, he'd be fired. He doesn't care. He's exhausted. His left ear is waterlogged. If Mr. Moneybags wants to rat on him, thinks Cam, let him. There are other jobs out there. If nothing else, he can go back to the car wash. If he's going to be wet and miserable, he'd at least like the satisfaction of watching shiny, clean cars drive off the lot.

"Take a ride with me in the magical mystery elevator," Welch says with a barker's flourish.

Why not? thinks Cam. He steps inside. Welch pushes number six.

"I was headed to the lobby to find Seymour, but I see I need to do a little public relations first."

"I'm not really interested in being your public relations project. Who's Seymour?"

"Our manager."

"Bald guy with a gray beard and glasses?"

"That's my Seymour. We call him the wizard."

"Your wizard's in the manager's office. They're adding up your bill, which apparently requires two accountants and a lawyer to calculate."

"You gotta love Seymour. He's our one-man fix-it crew. Whatever happens, Seymour comes in and opens his checkbook and makes all the goblins disappear."

"Must be nice."

"OK, kid. I'm all ears. You've got a load on your mind. Go ahead and dump it on me—I can take it."

"What if you hit somebody with one of your flying TV sets?"

"I have a look-out. I never toss anything out a window unless I get the all-clear from Bernie. Not only is he the meanest drummer in the business, he's got the eyes of an eagle. Next question."

"Have you ever cleaned up after yourself—ever?"

"Dude, you sound like my mother. She was always telling me to pick up my room. If she couldn't convince me, nobody can."

Cam doesn't even try not to roll his eyes in disgust.

"Look—I'm not the total asshole you have me pegged for. Is this really all you want to talk about? You've got the undivided attention of *Rolling Stone*'s pick for the greatest living rock guitarist and all you wanna know is do I ever pick up my own mess? Kid, you know how much insurance I carry on these?" He stretches out his fingers and wiggles them.

Cam doesn't know why he does what he does next. It's totally out of character for him. Crazy. Insane. He grabs both of Welch's hands in his, interlocking their fingers. He squeezes them just enough to let Welch know he can break them if he wants. It's suddenly clear to both of them how much bigger and stronger Cam is. In fact, Welch is a shrimp. On stage, he somehow gives the illusion of a giant figure, but Cam puts him at roughly 5' 5", 5' 7" tops, and maybe 140 pounds after a big spaghetti dinner.

"OK," he cries, "OK, OK, OK. Duuuude," he draws out the vowel as if in pain. "Believe me, you don't want to do this." Welch takes a deep breath and relaxes his fingers, and Cam simply holds them in place, firmly intertwined in his, but only applying as much pressure as he needs to keep Welch's attention. The elevator is slowly climbing upward. Through the speaker in the ceiling floats the happy tune of "On the Good Ship Lollipop."

Welch says, "OK, just tell me what you want. It's not a problem. If I can't get it for you, Seymour can. I mean it, kid—anything. We have enough coke up in the room to choke a rhino. Let's do a few lines together. There are women in there who will do *anything* to make you happy."

"Is there anyone in your life who can say no to you?"

"Look, OK, I'm an arrogant, selfish prick. It comes with the territory. But I'm obliged to milk this for whatever it's worth."

Cam tightens his grip on Welch's fingers.

"OK, OK," he says between clenched teeth. "Look—everybody I meet wants what I have—freedom, wealth, fame. Clapton has gone Disney on us. Somebody has to keep the freak flag waving."

"You can do better."

"What the hell does that mean? Of course I can do better. Everybody can do better. Do you want me to tell you how much money I give to charity—will that make you loosen your grip? What-do-you-want?"

Cam lets go of his hands. Welch is shocked and relieved. He lowers his hands, clinching and releasing his fingers, getting the blood flowing to them again. He shakes them out. "Look—I'm sure you're a righteous dude. Sorry I pissed you off. I sometimes have that effect on people. Normally, I would give you a fistful of concert tickets, but we're flying to Phoenix today. Who knows when we'll be back?"

Over the elevator speaker, Shirley Temple sings about bon bons and peppermints. Cam wipes the sweat off his palms with the towel. "I'm sorry," Cam says, "I got carried away. I haven't slept in a while." He inserts his pinky into his left ear and wiggles it.

"Hey, no harm, no foul. Let's ride this back down to the lobby. Seymour's got a suitcase full of money. Let me give you something for your trouble—"

Cam hits the stop button on the number pad. "You still don't get it. It's not about money." They are paused between the fifth and sixth floor.

"Everything is about money. I mean maybe not literally. But it's all about value. People place such a high value on my ability to play guitar, they're not only willing but happy to let me do whatever the hell I want, so long as I play. But if I stop playing, I lose my value. See—money."

"There's no way you're more valuable than Jimmy or Juan Carlos or a million others. You're just wrong about that. Somebody has to say it. That's just totally fucked up."

"You're an unusual kid. I like you."

Cam leans back against the paneling. Shirley Temple finishes her song with a peal of giggles. Frank Sinatra begins "Come Fly with Me." Welch looks up at the speaker. "Hey, it's Frank," he says. "I love that guy."

"What?—you love Frank Sinatra? He's so—"

"He's a classic, man. A classic never goes out of style. I'll bet Frank trashed his share of hotel rooms. With the Rat Pack in Vegas—are you kidding? They owned that town. They had total carte blanche. Frank was rock'n'roll before there was rock'n'roll."

"I can't picture him tossing TV sets into swimming pools."

"You ever see the Errol Flynn movie *The Adventures of Robin Hood*?"

"You're going to tell me Errol Flynn trashed hotel rooms? This isn't helping your case."

"My mom took me to see that movie at an art house in Santa Monica when I was about twelve. She was between husbands, and she thought we ought to spend some quality time together. When I saw that movie, I knew how to pursue my dream—disregard authority, chase pretty girls, feast like there's no tomorrow. And there it is—the rock'n'roll lifestyle."

"You missed a few essentials. Robin Hood fought for justice, not the right to party. He stole from the rich to help the poor, and he supported rightful authority by advocating the return of King Richard. Do you really believe people think of you as Robin Hood?"

"I look pretty good in tights."

"If anything, you're Prince John, the selfish tyrant who craves power without responsibility."

"What are you—nineteen going on forty-five? When I was your age all I wanted was to play in a band. Can we hit the button now and restart this thing? I have a plane to catch."

"You own the plane. It won't leave without you."

"Kid, I'm trying to be a nice guy here. I'm sorry you had to clean up my mess. I'm totally willing to pay you for your troubles."

"OK—what's my value?"

Welch sniffs and rubs his nose. "Name it."

"I want to hear you name it."

"Look—I'm pretty sure that if we get technical here, what you're doing is called kidnapping. I've got two bodyguards the size of gorillas upstairs. One word from me and they're on you, kid. I've seen their work. It's not pretty. You've had a hard morning. For—what now?—the third or fourth time?—I'm sorry. Let me do something for you. If you don't want money, OK, name it."

The truth is Cam has no idea what he wants. This wasn't his plan. There was no plan. He realizes that his lame attempt to teach morality to a perpetual adolescent is futile. Cam pushes the button; the elevator continues upward. "I want to see your suite."

"That's it? You haven't seen these rooms?"

"We're not allowed in the Royal Suite. We're not allowed on the sixth floor."

"Well, now you are."

The elevator dings and the doors slide open. Welch leads the way down the hall. The carpet is red up here, not chartreuse like it is on every other floor. The lighting fixtures are chandeliers, not cheap sconces. There are original paintings on the walls, but they have been defaced with black markers: Stick figures with oversized penises pee into tranquil country streams; dialogue bubbles with scribbled lyrics from the band's latest album have been drawn above the heads of people in the paintings. The closer they get to the wide-open double doors at the end of the hall, the more damage and debris clutter the place.

Inside the spacious living room, the lights are blazing. The band's drum set occupies the center of the room; chairs and couches have been piled against a far wall. Guitars litter the room. A topless young woman in huge Elton John glasses plunks individual keys on an electronic keyboard. Voices, male and female, drift in from another room in the suite. In the corner beside the doors, a TV set is turned to the Saturday morning cartoons. Scooby and the gang are driving through a storm towards a dark house on a hill. A bolt of lightening hits the peak of the house; partners in fear, Scooby and Shaggy embrace and shiver.

Cam walks across the room to the window. The glass has been completely shattered out, and the morning breeze blows the silk curtains from side to side. He looks down at the pool, which is clear of humans and debris. Cam looks back at the TV set.

A smile spreads across Welch's face. "Be my guest," he says.

Cam crosses the room and pulls the plug from the wall. His pool towel drops to the floor as he hoists the heavy RCA into a chest embrace. He picks up speed the closer he gets to the window. He launches it through. The sound that follows is part crash, part splash. Cam and Welch stand at the window together and survey the damage. There appears to be some debris on the cement patio next to the diving board. There are large pieces of the TV on the bottom of the deep end, near the drain.

"Fucking A!" shouts Welch, lifting his arms in mock triumph. "You hit water on your first TV, kid." He holds his hand out. Cam reaches out to shake it and Welch withdraws it. "Now eat my shit and die." Welch turns his back on Cam and walks into the adjoining room. Stunned, Cam hears a string of profanity from the other room. He hears Welch bark the order to hide the coke and call the cops. Given the tone of voice, it occurs to him that Welch is rousing his bodyguards.

Cam takes off running. The woman at the keyboard slurs, "Nice work." He knocks over pieces of the drum set on his way past, leaving a wake of booms and crashes. As he is running, Cam can hear the woman's voice behind him. "Was that really your first TV toss?"

Luckily, the elevator car is still on the sixth floor. When he pushes the button, the doors immediately slide open. Inside, he pushes the button for the basement. He hears a ruckus down the hall. Welch's goons are coming for him. He hits the button three, four times. He hears voices drawing closer and the sound of feet approaching. The doors begin to slide shut. Cam pushes his back up against the paneling. As the doors close, he hears another string of profanity and loud banging on the closed metal doors. But the elevator is descending.

The music now drifting through the elevator speaker above his head is Judy Garland singing "Life is Just a Bowl of Cherries." He thinks, *Well, that's it for this job. Good riddance. No more diving for televisions.* And then he realizes that Welch won't stop there. He might just have Cam arrested. He and his wizard Seymour could very well press charges for kidnapping or assault. Who knows? They might label him in the press as a stalker. His boss might—no, there's no *might* about this—his boss will prosecute for material damages. You can toss TVs out the window all day long if you're Juju Welch, greatest living rock guitarist, but the law is unforgiving for saps like him.

Judy sings, "You work, you save, you worry . . ." The numbers light up over the doors—four, three. He imagines Seymour and the hotel manager and the security guards waiting for him when the elevator opens. He looks at the ceiling. Is there an escape hatch? Is that even a real thing or is that just in the movies? He wonders if the cops will allow him to change into his clothes before they take him into custody. Sitting in a jail cell in a wet swimsuit would be the whipped cream topping to his fudge sundae morning. He smacks his left ear; it finally drains. The water tickles his lobe, and his hearing instantly improves. There's just a mild ringing now. Or is that Judy Garland's voice?

He briefly imagines himself hitting the stop button, climbing out through the shaft, crawling through the air ducts, and somehow finally riding his bike through the back streets of LA, laughing at the big jerk—at all the big jerks who rule the world.

"Wiggle your ears," sings Judy, "and think nothing of it..." The numbers over the doors light up—two, one. He sits on the floor in the middle of the elevator. He thinks about the TV, the one he tossed out the window, imagines it falling in slow motion, falling and falling from the Royal Suite, crashing into the wall of the deep end, shattering and sinking. There's one mess, he thinks, I will not have to clean up. Overhead, the letter B, for basement, brightens and glows, the elevator bell announces his arrival, and the doors slide open.

LESS RATTLE, MORE HUM

R ONNY BARLOW AWOKE TO THE VOICES OF TWO ORDERLIES
standing over the foot of his hospital bed. Through the beads of condensation on the inside of the oxygen tent, he could see them taking fresh sheets and blankets from the linen cart and setting them next to his legs, as they had done each morning at about the same hour. But today they took the remote control from its place on the bed rail and turned on the television news.

The TV set was suspended from the wall opposite his bed. After breakfast he would usually turn to the local station to watch reruns of *Father Knows Best* and *Leave It to Beaver* and *Dennis the Menace* and *I Love Lucy*. But it was too early for TV. The nurses didn't allow the set to be turned on until after his breakfast tray had been taken away. Something was different today. The hallway lights seemed brighter than usual, and the hustle and bustle at the nurse's station across the hall was noisier and more frantic. The orderlies had so far taken little notice of Ronny; their attention was focused on the flickering black and white images.

Ronny recognized the young man on the TV screen. He was giving a speech. He had given many speeches lately. He smiled a big-toothed smile to the large crowd who was cheering him on. One hand swept aside the shock of sandy hair that had fallen across his forehead, and the other hand flashed two fingers at the crowd—the peace sign. The unkempt hair and the peace sign set him apart from Ronny's parents. This was the candidate they were *not* going to vote for in the upcoming election. Ronny wondered, if he were old enough, would he vote for this young man or the older man who slicked his hair straight back like his father and whose chin was shadowed by heavy black whiskers that needed shaving.

The next picture recorded some loud popping noises that sounded to Ronny like firecrackers; the camera swept quickly over the crowd. The candidate with the big-toothed smile was laid out on the floor. Women were screaming. Then the news reporter appeared and explained that the man had been rushed to Good Samaritan Hospital. "It is upon the skill of doctors there and the grace of God," the reporter intoned, "that the hopes of many now hang."

One of the orderlies was much taller than the other. He spoke across Ronny's bed to the shorter one: "Shot in the damn head. Just like his brother."

Clipboard tucked under her arm, the morning nurse Ronny didn't like entered the room and looked up at the screen. "Any new information?" she asked.

"The shooter is an Arab with a funny name," answered the tall orderly. "They say Rosey Grier tackled the guy and held him down until the cops got the cuffs on him." All three gazed up at the screen until it went to commercial.

Noticing Ronny was awake, the nurse turned off the TV and opened the window blinds. "Let's see how that new IV is holding up." She checked the drip flow on the IV bottle hanging behind Ronny's bed. Then she turned the dial on the oxygen tank until the soft hissing sound stopped. She folded the plastic oxygen tent up over its metal frame. She picked up Ronny's hand and checked for bruising or swelling. The nurse had sunk a new needle into a fresh vein on the back of his left hand yesterday because the one in his right hand had moved and caused his hand to swell like a water balloon. "Looks good," she said. "Is it sore?"

Ronny shook his head. "What happened on the TV?"

"Oh, nothing," the nurse answered. "Just more grown up troubles. The world is full of them these days. Be glad you're still a boy. You needn't concern yourself with such things." She tucked the clipboard into the side rail, took her stethoscope from around her neck, and listened to Ronny's chest. "I do believe that wheeze is better today. Doctor Cassidy will be in later this morning."

"Will I go home today?" Ronny asked.

"Oh, good Lord, no," the nurse said, with the sour expression Ronny hated. It was the kind of face some grown-ups use to tell you how stupid and childish you are being. "Not today. And probably not tomorrow. But one of these days." She rehung the stethoscope around her neck. "I saw the breakfast trays out in the hallway. Are you hungry?"

"Sort of." Ronny imagined his usual bowl of Rice Krispies moistened with Mocha Mix, dry toast, orange juice, and applesauce—same thing every morning.

She stuck the thermometer under his tongue and held his wrist while she watched the second hand on her watch tick round. The other nurses still talked to you while they kept count of your pulse, but not this nurse. And she never mentioned the numbers like the others did. If you asked the others what your pulse was, or your temperature, they would tell you. Not this one. This nurse made you feel like you were a white rat in a science experiment.

When she finished writing the numbers onto her clipboard, she pulled the thermometer from his mouth, checked it, and shook it out. "I'd like to see you eat more today, and not just popsicles, real calories." She nodded to the orderlies on her way out. They scooted him to one side of the bed while they stripped the damp sheets and blankets from the other side. Then they scooted him onto the fresh, dry sheets while they finished changing the bed. It was a neat way they had of changing the bed while you were still in it. The tall orderly was having trouble shaking the news. He pursed his lips and made the same noise Ronny's grandma made in her throat when it became clear that she had lost her Solitaire game. And then just under his breath as he tucked the fresh sheets under the mattress: "Shot in the damn head."

By the time they were finished, and wheeling the linen cart out the door, the kitchen lady came in with his breakfast tray. She usually had a riddle for him: What has a face and two hands but no arms and legs? What gets wetter as it dries? There were no riddles today. Her eyes were red around the lashes and moist like Ronny's mother's eyes after she spoke to Dr. Cassidy.

The lady set the tray on the table and wheeled it into place. She lifted the cover and cleared her throat. "Eat hearty, my dear," she said. "Nurse Jones wants more meat on your bones by sundown."

They were always telling him to eat more, but the medicine made his stomach burn, and food seemed to make it worse. Some days it was hard to stifle the gag reflex. On days when his mother shoveled it in by the spoonful, he had to play a little mental game with himself to keep from coughing it back up. He called the game, "I'm not here." He couldn't remember when he had started the game, but it came in handy during certain painful procedures and also when the doctors and nurses surrounded his bed and talked about him in the third person. In his mind, he was at Knott's Berry Farm or Disneyland or the beach or the movies. Anywhere but here.

HIS FATHER WAS pacing the floor, smoking ferociously. There was some sort of trouble again between father and mother, and Ronny was at the center of it. Often, when he was supposed to be in bed, he crouched behind the banister at the top of the stairs, listening. When he peeked, he could see his mother seated at the kitchen table and his father's feet going up and back, up and back. The ashtray on the table had several spent cigarettes in it, some white butts stained with his mother's red lipstick, some brown butts that his father had snuffed out just above the filter. Two coffee cups and the coffee pot sat next to the telephone.

In the living room, the record had ended but neither his father nor his mother seemed to notice. They had turned on the record to cover their voices. What they didn't know was how their voices carried up the stairs even if Andy Williams was singing his heart out. If Ronny sat right here, in the spot where the stairs began their descent, with his bare feet pulled up beneath his pajamas, he could hear and not be seen.

His father spoke: "There's nothing more that can be done. You heard very well what the man said."

Then his mother: "I don't see any harm in a second opinion."

"Will you be satisfied by a second opinion? Or a third? Or a fourth?"

"When it's your son, you try everything. You don't stop until you've tried everything."

"Hasn't he been through enough? More hospitals, more needles, more tests, more time away from us—what will these things achieve? You heard what the man said. He knows what he's talking about."

"He also said it was a difficult diagnosis."

"And what do you think he meant by that?"

"You're saying he put it that way to soften the blow."

"You know he did."

"I won't give up."

"I'm not asking you to give up. I'm asking you to be realistic. Obviously we'll do everything we can to make him comfortable and happy. His life will be as normal as we can make it. But it's not normal. It never has been normal."

"I'm sorry if I'm making this harder for you."

"You don't have anything to be sorry about."

"I'm just not as logical as you are. To me it just doesn't follow that a series of tests determines his fate. He's a boy, not a math problem."

"Are you saying the doctors are lying?"

"Of course not."

"Then what? What are you saying?"

"When he has an attack and we take him in, and they give him the medicine and they give him the breathing treatments, he gets better. You've seen him. His color comes back. He eats. He sleeps. He grows stronger. He comes home."

"What the man was trying to tell us in so many words was that there will soon come a time when the medicine won't give the same results."

"So many words." Her cigarette lay on the edge of the ashtray. It had become a trail of gray ashes. Soon the ashes would break off and drop into the tray and the butt would fall backwards onto the kitchen table. His mother would grab the butt and snuff it out.

"Have you noticed the other kids at the bus stop?"

"Are you going to tell me again how big and healthy the neighbor kids are? Yes, I've seen the other kids. They're gaining weight. They're growing taller. Ronny's thin and frail. I see this. I'm his mother. I notice."

Ronny saw his father move closer to his mother. He heard his voice turn softer. "Let's have your mother come and stay with him this weekend. Let's get away for a day or two. Shall we drive up the coast?"

"I can't leave him now."

"He's fine."

"Tell me you didn't just say he's fine."

"Honey."

"Don't touch me. Don't try and soothe me. He's my boy. I need to feel this pain. I need to *feel* it. "

He heard his father go out the kitchen door. He peeked and saw his mother with her head on the table. Her cigarette was all gray ashes. Sure enough, the butt broke away from the ashes and fell back onto the tabletop. But his mother didn't take any notice of it. He got up and went back to his bedroom.

Standing at his window, Ronny watched his father carry the garbage cans from the side yard to the curb. He lugged the first can to the curb and slammed it down hard on the sidewalk. Its lid fell off and clanged into the street. His father marched back to the side yard. Ronny heard the metallic banging of the lid on the second can. Then his father had the heavy second can by its handles; he dragged it up the driveway. The can was too heavy; his father dropped it. He took two steps back from the trashcan. He put his hands on his hips and stared at it. He kicked the can and watched as the week's garbage spilled out onto the driveway. There were milk bottles and butcher wrappers and empty cereal boxes and soda bottles and beer cans and crinkled cigarette cartons. His father kicked the can again, putting a dent into its side. Ronny's father walked over to the first can and kicked it into the street. The garbage spilled out across the asphalt. Ronny saw his father put his hands on his hips. His body was bent at the waist, as if he were catching his breath.

His mother was coming up the stairs. He dove into bed and pulled the covers up to his chin. She was coming into his room. He turned onto his side and closed his eyes. His mother filled the room with her perfume and the smell of her cigarettes and her hairspray. She sat on the bed and put her hand on Ronny's forehead. He tried to control his breathing but couldn't; he was wheezing again. She leaned down and put her ear to his lungs, just as the doctor had instructed. The smell of her hairspray filled his nostrils; he tried to hold his breath.

At that moment, there was another crash of the cans down in the street. His mother crossed to the window, where she stood with her hand over her mouth. Ronny's eyes were open now. It was dark in his bedroom except for his nightlight and the moonlight coming in through the window. The moonlight spilled over his mother's face and head, making her hair shine the way Saint Catherine's hair shone in a painting at the church where he had been baptized. His mother watched his father. His father had once been surprised by a skunk while putting out the garbage. Was there another skunk out there? His mother's breath came in gulps, just as Ronny's did during the early phase of one of his attacks. He sat up in bed. She turned to face him.

"It's all right," she said. "Lie back and relax. Everything is all right."

"I'm not stupid," he said. "I'm just a boy, but I'm not stupid."

"Of course you're not," his mother said. "You're the smartest person I know."

"What happened to the man who was shot?"

"He died. He was killed. Assassinated, they call it."

"Why was he assassinated?"

"A crazy man . . . a man who isn't right in the head . . . it's hard to explain."

"I want to know. Everybody keeps telling me not to worry. But people are upset. Things are happening in the world that are not safe. The world is changing, isn't it?"

Half of his mother's face was in the blue light now, and the other half was in shadow. "I don't think it is. I think the world is going on more or less as it always has. But sometimes it seems harder for us to all live together. Things get worse for a time, and then they get better again. I'm not sure why. I'm pretty sure it's the way it's always been. Nothing really changes. It's all in how you look at things."

"But there's a war now. That makes things different."

"In some ways, yes. In some ways, no."

"When Dad was in the other war, in Korea, what did you do?"

"I didn't know your dad then. We didn't meet until after he came home from the war. He was working for the Edison Company and so was I. But we didn't know each other. And then one day, your dad came into the office where I sat at a desk all day and answered the phone. He was a handsome man, tall, dark. He wore his hair flat on the top and combed it back on the sides. That was how some of the popular singers were wearing their hair then. He sat down on the edge of the desk and lit up a cigarette. I thought he looked like Frank Sinatra."

"And what did he say to you?"

His mother sat on the corner of the bed. "He said, 'I've just been hired in outside sales at Traveline Metals. Next Friday will be my last day of work here. So I think you and I should get acquainted before I leave and we never see each other again.'"

"And what did you say?"

"I said, 'Congratulations on your new position. But I don't think my fiancé would like it very much if you and I got acquainted in quite that way.'"

"That's not the end of the story."

"No. He went home and wrote me a letter that night. Next morning, the letter was on my desk when I came into work."

"What did the letter say?"

"It listed all the reasons that I should break it off with my fiancé and go out with him."

"And you did."

"Not right away. I waited a respectable two days."

"That must've been quite a letter."

"Yes, sir, it was. Nobody had ever said anything to me in that way before. I thought if he were sincere, if the things in that letter were really the things in his heart, then I couldn't marry anyone else."

"So you told the other fellow to hit the road, Jack, don't come back."

"I'll let you in on a little secret. There was no other fellow. No one to compare anyway. Your father swept me off my feet."

"Does that mean he was a good dancer?"

"He was a good dancer. Still is. But it means more than just dancing."

"Dr. Cassidy said I would be dancing the jig again soon. What's the jig?"

"It's a happy dance. When did he say that?"

"When he released me to come home. He said I could come home *for now*. Does that mean I'm going back to the hospital?"

"It means you're home now."

"If I had just come home from the war, would I be able to have ice cream for breakfast?"

"What put that notion into your head?"

"Dad told me once that he had ice cream for breakfast when he got home from the war. I thought that meant you gave it to him."

"No, I guess Grandma gave it to him."

"What flavor do you suppose he had?"

"Chocolate, I guess. I've never known him to eat another flavor."

"And he eats it so slow. I can't eat ice cream that slow. It gets all melty."

"He likes it that way."

"Can I have some chocolate ice cream for breakfast?"

She brushed the sandy hair on his forehead aside with her fingers. "I guess so."

"Do we have some in the freezer?"

"I'll send your father out for some. But you need your sleep. Somebody who's going to eat chocolate ice cream for breakfast needs at least eight hours of sleep first."

"You don't think somebody will shoot Dad, do you?"

"No. There's no reason for somebody to shoot your dad."

"People shot at him in the war."

"The war is over. Nobody will shoot at him anymore."

"The war is over but there are assinations."

"Assassinations. That's different. You don't have to worry about that."

"Well, then, what should I worry about?"

His mother stood up and moved back to the window. She held her hand up to her forehead and rubbed it back and forth with the tips of her fingers. "I'll let you know," she said. "There must be a few good things for a smart boy like you to worry about. Shall I make you a list?"

"Make me a list like the list Dad made for you. Make me a worry list and put it on the table in the morning, and I'll read it while I eat my chocolate ice cream."

"Turn over and let me listen to your chest."

"It's fine now. I was wheezing earlier, but I'm fine now."

She put her ear to Ronny's back and listened to his breathing. The soft rattle in his lungs was like the sound of wind through dry leaves. But his breath was steady and unlabored. She kissed his forehead and left the room.

He could feel a damp spot on his thin baseball pajamas where her cheek had been. He knew, even though he couldn't see it, that there was a reddish smear of lipstick on his forehead. He raised his hand up to catch some of the moonlight. The same soft, blue light that had lit his mother's face now lit the palm of his hand. He lowered the hand and held his palm against his cheek. He lay still for several minutes before he heard his father's car start up and pull out of the driveway.

He imagined his father pulling into the parking spot right in front of the drugstore, buttoning his cardigan as he swung the heavy car door shut, and waving to the bald man at the checkout counter as the bell over the door clanged. His father would walk to the freezer in the back of the store and pull an icy carton from the case. He would talk to the man at the cash register in his deep salesman's voice. How was business? How were his wife and daughter? What chances did he think the Dodgers had of a pennant this season?

Ronny turned onto his stomach and listened to his breath. He was not coughing. He could hear the phlegm rattling around in his lungs. If he could spit it all up, once and for all, that might be the end of it. He wouldn't need to play the game. He could be here always. Here at home. Where he belonged.

In the morning, Ronny would be treated just like a soldier home from the war. The sun would be shining through the branches of the plum tree and onto the kitchen table. There would be a bowl of chocolate ice cream before him and his favorite spoon—the one with Bugs Bunny on the handle. And he would have a list to organize the worry that had been swirling around him.

THE RESPIRATORY THERAPIST Ronny loved entered the hospital room, pushing his wheeled machine into place next to Ronny's bed. He was a young man with wild red hair, crooked front teeth, and a string of love beads around his neck. In a mildly exaggerated imitation of Alfred Hitchcock, he intoned, "Good eve-a-ning."

"It's afternoon," Ronny said, suppressing a smile.

The therapist slowly walked towards the window and raised the blinds. "So it is." He gazed outside. The window looked out over a cemetery with rows of upright stone slabs planted in a perfect lawn. The young man hunched his shoulders and rubbed his palms together. "And this," he switched to his Peter Lorre voice, "is where we bury our mistakes." He grinned his evil little grin, turning toward Ronny.

Ronny couldn't help giggling. "Do you make a lot of mistakes?" he asked.

The therapist played his part well, allowing the grin to widen and overtake his face. "Only when the moon is full and the wolfsbane is in bloom." His nose twitched.

Ronny giggled harder. He was sitting up in bed now. He started to cough and laugh. "And . . . what . . . happens then?"

The therapist crouched, mussing his hair with his fingers. He howled, beginning with a low moan and a snarl, then a long, open-throated wolf call. Ronny laughed and coughed. The therapist straightened his spine and ran a comb through his hair, stepped to one side, and said in a refined British accent, "Igor, what are you doing?"

The therapist took a step aside and crouched again, saying breathily, "Nothing, master." He stood upright and said, "You must run down to the moat and feed the piranha!" He crouched. "Yes, master," he whispered, shuffling behind the nebulizer machine.

"You changed it," Ronny said. "You changed it to Cary Grant!"

"Very good," said the therapist. "Well, I had to, after what you said about my Jimmy Cagney."

Ronny was still laughing and coughing. The therapist handed him the plastic vomit pan. "Spit it up," he said.

Ronny cleared his throat and produced some phlegm into the container. "You mixed up your Edward G. Robinson with your Jimmy Cagney."

Shifting quickly into his Jimmy Durante, he said, "Ev-rybody's a critic!"

Ronny laughed and coughed and produced more sputum.

"Hey, good job. I think I'll keep Durante."

"You don't have the nose for it." Ronny took a tissue and wiped his lips.

The therapist unwound the electrical cord and plugged it into the socket. "All right, my friend, that's a good start. Let's see if we can loosen up that crud and—do you remember the fancy word for spitting up?"

"Expectorate," Ronny said.

"Expectorate a little, brother."

Ronny coughed up a bit more.

"You remember my good friend, Mr. Nebulizer." He hooked up the tubing, connected a new plastic mouthpiece to it, and flipped on the switch to the air compressor. The machine began to hum and hiss.

Ronny swung his legs over the edge of the bed and held onto the mouthpiece as the red-headed therapist injected the clear liquid into the medicine cup.

"All right, you told me you were a music fan, so . . . " He took hold of the transistor radio that Ronny's mother had left on his nightstand. "I thought we'd run a little experiment." He turned on the radio and tuned it to a rock 'n' roll station. "Let's see if we can get a little rhythm going." He turned the tuning nob until The Lemon Pipers' song "Green Tambourine" came in clearly. Soon the medicine vaporized and began to emerge through the mouthpiece in an even mist. Ronny placed the mouthpiece between his lips and inhaled deeply. The therapist snapped the nose clip into place. "Now, just listen to the music and breath in time. That's it, take it slow now."

Ronny closed his eyes and concentrated on the music. After a few deep breaths, he opened his eyes. The therapist was standing in the middle of the room waving his arms fluidly like a conductor. Ronny laughed and coughed. Between the laughter and the rhythm of the music, Ronny was able to cough up more than his usual amount. He might be able to get some sleep tonight. He would eat a few popsicles and listen to the Laker game on the transistor and possibly drift off and not awaken until the midnight nurse came in to take his temperature and listen to his chest. He would fall asleep to the squeak of sneakers on the wooden floor and the cheers of the crowd and the impassioned narration of Chick Hearn calling the game from center court in the fabulous Forum.

"I *thought* I heard music in here." The young, blond nurse who came on duty in the afternoons stood in the doorway. She stepped inside and closed the door to Ronny's room. Like the girls on *American Bandstand*, she danced across the room toward the respiratory therapist, who turned to Ronny with his best Harpo Marx take, honking an imaginary horn as he joined the nurse in a dance. Ronny breathed in the medicine until the song was finished. Then he pulled the mouthpiece away and coughed and spat.

Another song started up, a slow one—Merrilee Rush's "Angel of the Morning." The young couple moved together, swaying a bit, the way Ronny's parents did when they danced in the living room to the Ray Conniff Singers. He had an arm around her waist, and she had a hand on his shoulder. Their opposite hands were clasped. Ronny breathed in the medicine deeply, in time with the song.

It was a pretty song. Ronny had heard it before, but not at home. It was not the sort of music his parents listened to on their hi-fi; however, his mom wouldn't turn the station if a song like that came on the radio in the car. It was a sad song, but a happy one at the same time. The sadness came from the part of the song that talked about leaving, and the happy part came from a sense that things would go on in spite of the leaving. Someone was touching someone's cheek in the morning, and that seemed to be the part of the song where the happy and the sad blended together.

As Ronny tried to picture the scene in his mind later that evening, it wasn't exactly clear how they all at once became aware of the older, mean nurse standing in the doorway, holding the door open wide. She had come to check on Ronny before leaving for the day. Although it startled them to see her there, the older nurse didn't look angry. In fact, she had a look on her face that Ronny had never seen before, as if she were remembering something from long ago. Her gaze was directed at the dancing couple but was unfocused. Her lips, usually pursed, were relaxed and slightly parted. Ronny thought she looked a little bit sleepy, as if she'd just awoken from a nap.

The respiratory therapist quickly snapped off the transistor radio. The young nurse straightened her uniform. The older nurse looked over at Ronny and said, "I've restocked the red popsicles." She turned back to the young nurse. "He doesn't like the orange ones, and he hates the green ones. Who can blame him? The orange ones just taste watery and the lime ones taste like medicine. Only the red ones will do." She turned to leave, then looked back. "Finish all the medicine in that machine, young man. I want to hear less rattle and more hum in those lungs come morning." The door swung closed.

The respiratory therapist and the nurse exchanged a confused look. Ronny understood that they expected to be in trouble. It was like the time his mother had come into his room when he was jumping on the bed. He thought he would get a spanking for sure. But all she did was tell him to change out of his pajamas because his tutor was downstairs.

And then something passed between the therapist and the nurse that Ronny wasn't able to comprehend. Except for the low rumble of the air compressor, there was a moment of complete silence in the room. Then the therapist adjusted the nurse's cap, which had fallen askew. Her heel had come out of her shoe during the dance. She stooped to slip it back on before she left the room. "You heard what nurse Jones said. Less rattle, more hum."

The red-headed therapist was unusually quiet as he packed up the nebulizer that afternoon. There were fewer jokes and movie star imitations than usual. Ronny breathed easier as he slid his legs back under the sheets and the therapist rolled the sides of the oxygen tent back down and tucked them under the edges of Ronny's bed covers. He flipped the switch on the wall, and the hiss of oxygen began to fill Ronny's tent once again.

"Should I worry about you?" Ronny asked.

"Why would you do that?"

"Nobody with hair like yours can avoid trouble for long."

"Was that John Wayne? Were you just doing John Wayne in my presence?" The therapist walked toward Ronny with Wayne's slip-hipped saunter. "Now, look, pilgrim, if there's worrying to do, I'll be the one to do it. This hospital ain't big enough for two worriers."

"I reckon we'll just have to solve that little problem the old-fashioned way." Ronny pulled his imaginary six-shooter from its holster and fired. The therapist grabbed his chest and dropped to his knees. Ronny blew the smoke from the end of his index finger.

The therapist sputtered, "Tell my mother . . . I'm sorry . . . I never . . . cleaned my room." He fell to the floor and lay still as Ronny giggled without coughing. He lay there quietly until Ronny's laughter ceased.

"I wish you were my big brother," Ronny said.

"I am your brother. We were waiting until your birthday to tell you."

"Were you going to vote for the man who got shot?"

"Yes, I was."

"What's going to happen now?"

"No one knows. People are more or less in shock."

"My mother says not to worry about it."

"Good advice. Worrying doesn't change anything. It just makes you feel worse."

"It makes me feel better."

"Does it? Why?"

Ronny thought for a minute. "I don't know. I can't see your chest moving. Are you still breathing?"

"Yes. You?"

"Yes."

"Let's keep it that way, shall we?" The therapist raised his wristwatch to his face. "I have to go to my next appointment." He stood and brushed off his trousers with his palms. He bared his teeth and hitched his thumbs in his belt. "Whaddaya think, shall I close the blinds?"

"I like your Bogart. The secret to Bogart is you can't overdo it. And you can't say 'Here's lookin' at you.' Everybody does that."

"I'll remember that. The blinds?"

"Leave them open. It gives me something to look at other than the TV."

"Deep breath."

Ronny drew in a long breath. When it reached its peak, he coughed.

The therapist wheeled his machine toward the door. "I passed the kitchen earlier. Smelled like pizza-flavored Jello."

"Will wonders never cease?"

"Save me one of those red popsicles."

"OK."

"Any requests for tomorrow?"

"Jimmy Stewart."

"The young, gangly Jimmy Stewart, who mugs for the camera, or the older, halting Jimmy Stewart who looks permanently conflicted?"

"Surprise me. But no *Harvey* speeches. Everybody does *Harvey*. Aim for *The Man Who Shot Liberty Valance*."

"It scares me how many movies you've seen."

"It's either that or homework."

"Quick. What's twelve times forty?"

"Four hundred eighty."

The therapist let his eyes grow big. He pushed the door and let it close on him, knocking him out into the hallway. Ronny giggled. He heard the young man singing "Green Tambourine" all the way down the outer hall, and he heard the nurses shushing him.

At home, this was his favorite time of the day, when he sat at the kitchen table as his mother organized dinner or chatted on the phone to her friends while he figured problems in his school workbooks or drew pictures with his colored pencils. But in the hospital, this was the most boring time of the day. There was a steady shuffling of nurses in the hallway as the shifts changed. The sky outside began to darken and his room also began to darken. His tent misted up and the condensation began to run down the inside of the plastic like rain on a window pane. He sometimes drew pictures in it with his index finger, but that only made the water drip on his sheets.

At dinnertime the kitchen lady would pop his light on as she delivered his tray. His father would stop in on his way home from work. Sometimes he would stay until eight o'clock, when visiting hours ended and everyone, even mothers and fathers, had to leave. Ronny would watch TV for a while, until it was time for popsicles and the Laker game.

Then came the long, lonely night. Often he lay awake. Sometimes there were strange feelings that came over him, and pains that struck him in his chest and in his stomach. The needle in the back of his hand ached. During these hours he cried out for his mother. He imagined her perfume and her laughter. He pictured her lipstick on the edge of her coffee cup. Sometimes one of the young nurses would hear him and use the excuse of checking his IV to hold his hand.

In his mind he would rerun a movie—either one of the old ones he'd seen on television or an Elvis Presley movie he'd seen recently in the theater. Or he would imagine he was riding the Matterhorn Bobsleds with his father. He would lean into the turns just as he did on the actual ride. He would imagine his father holding him tightly. Sometimes he remembered his father reading to him from the Golden Book, *Little Boy with a Big Horn*. It was his favorite bedtime story, about a little boy named Ollie who played one song over and over again on the tuba. Ronny's father sang the words to the song in his deep, bellowing voice, going especially low at the end, like the low notes on a tuba: "There are many brave hearts asleep in the deep."

His father had been brave in the Korean War. His grandma had said so. She said he had won medals for bravery, like the medal the mayor of the town pinned on young Ollie at the end of the story because his tuba playing warned boats in the fog to avoid the rocks. But Ronny's father only changed the subject when Ronny asked him about it. He would like to see those medals some day. Where did his father keep them?

When he got home, he would go looking for them in his father's drawers. There were lots of things in his drawers—hats and watches and neckties from the old days. He also kept some of his army things in a box in the garage. Ronny had seen his father rummaging through it once. His uniform was in there, and some photographs, and some letters he had written to his parents from the veteran's hospital after it was all over. Ronny would find them when he got home.

Gauguin's Razor

December 23, 1888, Arles, France

Neighbors

THE ENTIRE NASTY INTERLUDE WITH MONSIEUR VAN GOGH came to a head the day the other crazy drunk stepped off the train—the one they call Gauguin. More than once the constable was called to escort the pair from Ginoux's café back to the butter-yellow house of Place Lamartine, from which erupted all manner of threats and accusations and fistfights.

Only later did we discover that van Gogh had wooed him here with promises of sunflowers and tobacco, women and booze. Perhaps, like all advertisement, it was merely artful exaggeration. Yet Gauguin swallowed the bait and allowed himself to be reeled in.

There is no need for us to overstate our case. Any reasonable person would object to their flagrant disrespect for the law. Oh, there were a few days there at the start when the two of them gleefully lugged their easels to the edge of the fields and returned at dusk with bright splotches of paint in their beards. Those days seemed peaceable enough for all concerned.

They were not to last. Perhaps it should be said that one cannot really blame Gauguin, who grew weary, as did we, of van Gogh's moods—the brooding clouds of anxiety and obsession, the lightning strikes of jealousy and anger. Let us be frank—where Monsieur van Gogh is concerned, it is much easier to live with the pictures than with the man himself.

All praise to the distant brother for keeping him in oils and brushes. His daily bread, however, came from us. The women of Arles fed him the way you would a caged animal—to keep him from striking.

We were not surprised when on that December night, one of them dripped blood through the streets. No one knows exactly what happened. To this day, most of us think Gauguin drew his razor. It would not have been out of character. But young Rachel received the wounded matador's offering, spreading the tall tale of self-mutilation.

The tragedy was followed by three days of hard rain. Within the yellow walls we heard weeping and splintering wood. When Gauguin boarded the train for Paris, we prayed van Gogh would follow. Yes, we signed the petition to evict. Any reasonable person would. We would each of us rather live with the pictures than the man.

One cannot really blame Gauguin. And surely we ourselves are not to blame for the problems of that redheaded madman. Some people manage to carry their troubles lightly. Some seethe with a restless fury that cannot be subdued. Over at the asylum in Saint-Remy, they said there were nights when he howled at the moon and ate paint. So many now think of his talent as a blessing; truly, it may have only been the husk of a curse. Certainly, no one who met him expected him to grow old. The haunted, swirling colors in his sky tell you that much.

Rachel

I WAS BEHIND the drawn curtain in the parlor with my Tuesday regular, who had brought us a bottle of plum brandy. We heard a fracas out in the street, which turned out to be Vincent's righteous neighbors shouting insults. When he came to the door, Madam Larousse placed her hand on Vincent's chest and spoke a few kind words to try and calm him. But his mind was in a state that words couldn't reach.

His face was streaked with tears and his sweater was ripped; it hung around his waist in shreds. Seeing the blood, Madam sent Cherie to fetch Dr. Rey. With eyes lowered, Vincent handed me a gift wrapped in newspaper. Naturally, I unwrapped it. When I realized what it was, I fainted. Our houseman Monsieur Rainer caught me and laid me on the divan.

When I came to, Vincent was pacing in front of the fireplace and Dr. Rey was just hanging up his hat. Monsieur Rainer offered me more brandy. "Vincent," I said. "Why?"

"Gauguin is leaving! He said he won't remain in Arles. Too provincial. And I am . . . I have . . . driven him away with my . . . my fits."

"Come here, my darling." He laid his head in my lap. Vomit came into my throat. I laid my scarf over the bloody flap of what remained. While Dr. Rey knelt and examined the wound, I turned my head away. Madam shooed the crowd. The young constable arrived with his notebook. Madam told him what she knew; he jotted notes. I breathed the way the midwife taught me to keep from fainting again.

But I fainted anyway, and Monsieur Rainer carried me upstairs, laying the folded newspaper on the table beneath the window. By morning the blood had dried, and it looked something like the mushrooms the monks gather in the forest.

I have never told anyone where I buried it.

Thereafter when I spotted Vincent, he couldn't make eye contact. Always his head cast down, his nervous hands like birds at his side, his shuffling gait. He was a man to be pitied, not a man to be adored.

The last time I saw him, he was headed toward the fields one morning, easel on his shoulder like a soldier's rifle. He spoke of wheat like waves on the ocean and a road that melted into the sun. He told me he was a crow, pecking at leftovers after harvest. He spoke that way when the curse was upon him. There was no succor for him in such moods. He said to me, "You were Gauguin's favorite."

When I reached out to touch the wound, he knocked my hand away and crossed the avenue. I might have followed, but Madam Larousse had sent me to fetch flowers for our table. I watched him walk away in that crooked way he always walked, as if half of him wanted to turn, and the other half to go straight.

Gauguin

MY DEAR BERNARD, I am leaving for Paris tomorrow to settle some matters with Theo van Gogh, who has sold three of my paintings. Apparently someone other than Monet and Renoir are now able to move the public. I will deliver six more canvases, all completed under great stress, with Vincent arguing with me through each stroke of the brush.

I cannot remain in Arles one moment more. The weather here is dreary, the mistrals cold and wet, and the town, such as it is, with the exception of one lovely whore, filled with dolts. The madness that visited Vincent in Paris has now taken up permanent residence in his skull. Our friend suffers in body, mind, and spirit. Worse, he has become a most pitiful object of ridicule and derision: the wicked urchins of this province follow him through the streets, pelting him with stones and provoking him to fits that I can only describe as demonic. The morning after the worst of these episodes, he became catatonic, unable to talk or eat, like a wounded animal cowering in the corner of its nest. Or like a housecat who crawls beneath the bed to die. I will recommend to Theo that he commit his brother to an asylum for his own safety.

Three nights ago we went to the local café for absinthe. Vincent had been on edge all day, and I thought a glowing glass of the Green Fairy might bring relief. He hurled his glass at me because of a comment I made to the owner's wife. You know the sort of comment I mean. I say things all the time. This was nothing out of the ordinary. We have both painted this woman's portrait, and I assumed that we had shared her in jest and good will, like an amiable whore. But I must have struck a jealous vein, and we ended up exchanging words. Perhaps we exchanged more than just words, for we found ourselves tangling in the street outside. I subdued him and returned to the café to further pursue my prey. Bernard, you know me when I am on the scent; I cannot be distracted or waylaid.

The next morning, Vincent was escorted back to his ridiculous yellow house by a uniformed fool, a bandage wrapped around his head as though he had just returned from the Prussian front. It is lucky you did not join us here after all. I will tell Theo what you said, Bernard, about how some of the young doctors have begun to specialize in maladies of the soul; perhaps there is hope for Vincent yet.

As for me, I have had my fill of "civilization." In spring I hope to depart for warmer climes, preferably Madagascar. Surely the future of painting is in the tropics, and I grow increasingly weary of domestic burdens. Travel is the only thing to jar me from this malaise. The savage will return to the wild. Why not join me?

Roulin

I NEVER UNDERSTOOD Vincent's love for Gauguin. The man was like a looming hurricane; when his havoc came ashore, it swept away every human feeling in its path. Many here said the same of Vincent, but not my Augustine and not my children and not me. He loved Augustine's fish stew, appearing at the kitchen window whenever the pot was on the stove. The portraits were his only way of repaying her for all the meals he devoured after my postal satchel was empty and after his hands began to ache from a day of furious strokes. This was our way with him: Augustine kept him fed; I kept him drunk. Before Gauguin arrived, many was the night I propped him up and hobbled him homeward.

But Gauguin—Gauguin would leave him sleeping in the street for the constable to find. There is no doubt Gauguin cut him, probably aiming for the throat.

Sometimes Vincent had me read Theo's letters aloud. Normally they soothed him. But on the morning of that fateful day, the letter set him to pacing. Usually news of a wedding in the family is received with joy. But Vincent was shaken, agitated. If I had to guess, I'd say he feared that a wife would mean fewer visits from Theo, and fewer parcels of his precious art supplies.

To make matters worse, when Gauguin awoke, he came outside holding one of Vincent's canvases. "If you could only learn how to hold your brush," he mocked, "these mangled sunflowers might make sense." Vincent wrested the picture from his grasp and set it back on the easel.

Late that night Dr. Rey appeared at our door. I was already awake, having heard the commotion down at Place Lamartine. He gave my Augustine and me some laudanum to see Vincent through, and we passed the hours of darkness at his side until dawn. Augustine settled the children and nursed Vincent, while I dosed him.

I am bigger than Gauguin, and I have no fear of him. I only wish I had hustled him away sooner. I was at the station collecting the mail from Paris the day he left. He jostled past me with Vincent's pipe in his teeth. I said to him, "Good riddance to bad garbage, thief." He snorted with a superior nod as he boarded the train.

The women of Arles called Gauguin "the beast." He looked the part and played it well, flaunting the conventions of village life. A man of appetites, he lived to drink and fight and fuck. Theo knew this well and cautioned his brother. But Vincent loved all creatures with a pure heart. And Theo—well, Theo was his junior. There are truths you can't hear from the lips of a brother, and there are secrets you can't confide in a brother's ear. But you can speak freely to a friend over absinthe . . . secrets passed between friends are a sacred trust, and I will keep Vincent's confessions to my grave.

Vincent

DEAR THEO, IT WILL no doubt settle your worries to know that I have attained some measure of serenity here, due in no small part to Dr. Peyron's insights about the nature of my malady—a kind of epilepsy that strikes the brain like a storm of fireworks, then leaves one paralyzed in a stupor for days afterward. The knowledge that mine is a disease that may be treated rather than a torment of my own dark choosing is a balm to me. The regimen here at Saint Paul's of regular if unremarkable meals, fresh air, and twice-weekly baths has set me on a steady course. Here there are no spying neighbors, no street boys throwing rocks and taunts, no police, and no creditors. I have been allowed to set up a small studio in one of the vacant rooms, and in the past twelve days I have begun a flurry of new pieces.

I am presently at work on a study of a starry sky above the sleepy town of Saint-Remy. Zola's "infinite depths" appear as fiery gems in the milky way. While at work this afternoon I unconsciously reached for my phantom ear and the disaster with Gauguin sprang to life again in my mind. Instead of reliving the tragedy anew, I looked through the window bars at the sky and thought of the Japanese monks, how they would simply enter the landscape and dwell there until the luminous spirit that animates all nature awakened their vision. I felt release from my obsession, and I returned my brush to the swirling strokes of a looming cypress, a dark echo of the flames burning in my sky. I have been staring at these trees since I arrived—the valley below is rife with them—but I have not truly *seen* them until now. Theo, it is as if I have been given a glimpse into eternity, so vivid is the pulse that moves through me. Dr. Peyron speculates that this state is a consequence of my epilepsy. When I said to him that I have always had this odd level of vision, in varying degrees, since our childhood in Zundert, he explained that I likely was born with the condition and recent stresses have called it forth in full measure.

But these brief ecstasies are fleeting. In the worst of it—when I am haunted at length by voices and delusions and violent impulses—I fear I may never recover equilibrium. And in these times I reach across the dark abyss for your open hand. It is to you, my dear brother, that I owe all the good, if any good at all, that has entered my otherwise tormented life.

My deepest congratulations and good wishes to you and Jo upon your marriage. I hope to be able to visit your new apartment and perhaps hang this new picture in a place where it would bring you both joy. Thank you for the parcel of colors; please send more when possible; already my supply grows sparse.

Theo

My Dearest Jo, This has undoubtedly been the hardest day of my life. The carpenter spent the morning building Vincent's coffin in the little room here where he had his studio, while the mortician was in the next room preparing my brother's body for burial. I spent those hours sorting through some of the new paintings, which I displayed around the billiard room here at Auberge Ravoux where we held the service. The room reeked of carbolic acid.

I was comforted by a few devoted representatives from our mutual circle of friends: Emile Bernard, Lucien Pissaro, the dealer Tanguy, and Dr. Paul Gachet, who treated my brother's wound. Gauguin was conspicuously absent. I cannot help but trace the beginning of Vincent's final struggle to Gauguin's stay in Arles two years ago.

I will never forgive myself for failing Vincent. You say I shouldn't blame myself, and I love you for wanting to protect me from guilt, but he was my brother, my flesh and blood. Why was I able to sell Gauguin's work, and Monet's, even Cezanne's, and not the splendid and unique work of my own dear brother? He wanted nothing more than a taste of their success, to be appreciated for the advances he made, and I wanted nothing more for him. Perhaps what he told me once is true after all: "My paintings will mature quietly like fine wine in a cellar." I cling to this hope for his sake.

Your brother Andries was a great help to me today. Together he and I led the procession to the burial site, a sunny spot amid the wheat fields. The entire company stood in the sweltering midday while Gachet said some words. We poured in the dirt. Gradually, the gracious company left me alone on the heath to weep. I lost track of time. Eventually, Andries fetched me as evening fell. He had already accompanied our guests to the train station. Tonight I have eaten a few bites and drunk some of the wine that Ravoux's daughter brought to our room. Andries and I will complete a few final tasks tomorrow and return to Paris the next day. Kiss little Vincent for me. I am gladder than ever we named him after his uncle but pray that his life is brighter and happier than that of his namesake.

Looking through Vincent's meager belongings, among the half-spent paint tubes and the still-wet canvases, I came across an unsent letter to Gauguin. In it my brother muses upon creation as a failed study made by the great Artist on a bad day, resulting in a world teeming with the beauty that only a Master could evoke, but damaged by His hurried strokes and ruined attempts at innovation, leaving us disappointed and wanting to see more of His work in order to judge it fairly. While our father would never approve of this theology, I cannot help but see it as Vincent's gentle attempt to forgive God for the broken life He produced. He ends the reverie by saying, "We must not take this life for anything but what it is, and go on hoping that in some other life we'll see something better than this."

Cole Porter and
the Sixth Moon

Time past and time future
What might have been and what has been
Point to one end, which is always present
—T. S. Eliot, *Four Quartets*

O N THE EVE OF ST. MICHAEL'S DAY, WHEN ABBOT LOUIS assigned me the task of fetching Brother Philip, I had the feeling I was being tested. As we filed out of chapel after noon prayers, our novice master, Brother Bartholomew, took me by the sleeve and guided me to the abbot's office. Across his big oak desk, Father Louis handed me a map and a compass. He walked me to the window and pointed in the direction of the tallest peak, explaining the contours of the terrain ahead of me. It was only seven miles as the crow flies, but the trail was mostly uphill and beneath a thick canopy of fir trees.

In the kitchen, Brother Bartholomew loaded a rucksack with a jar of tap water and a fresh barley loaf still warm from the oven. To this he added the map and the compass. Then he took me to the barn and pulled down from a high shelf a box filled with clothing. After a brief postulancy, a new monk becomes a novitiate, which is when he surrenders his street clothes and dons the habit of the order. There in the barn is where the street clothes are stored. Bartholomew pulled from the box a thick pair of wool socks. Then he got a ladder and brought down from the rafters a box of donated shoes. Inside were hiking boots of various sizes. "See if any of these fit," he said, placing my regulation sandals on the lower shelf of the potting table.

"I don't suppose you were ever a Boy Scout?" he asked.

"Only long enough to earn three merit badges and sew a summer jamboree patch on my shoulder," I answered.

"You passed the compass test?"

"Of course."

"Then you're already ahead of Brother Timothy, who got lost in the woods last year." He grinned the same crooked, mildly sadistic grin he wore when passing out written exams to our theology class. "Don't worry," he said, "the rangers found him on the second day of searching, only a mile off course." He chuckled. "A little worse for the wear."

"I don't believe I've met Brother Timothy," I said.

"No, and you're not likely to. Soon as he got rehydrated, he made a bee-line for the bus station. He's now a community college English teacher in Boise."

When I was suitably outfitted, Brother Bartholomew walked me to a seldom-used gate at the rear of the herb garden, which consisted of a mass of splinters that squeaked open on rusty hinges. The sound of that gate still echoes down these many years. It would make an excellent sound effect for any horror movie featuring an eerie old house. He ushered me through the gate and latched it behind me.

As Brother Bartholomew slid the bolt back into place, I paused there, on the nether side of the garden gate, to hike up the rucksack on my shoulders and consider: Had I been sent on a mission, or had I been exiled? No angel waved a flaming sword to keep me out, but I had the distinct feeling that I had been evicted from Paradise.

At that time I knew practically nothing about the man I had been sent after. Widely-known outside Olivet Abbey as Trevor Mason, a poet and writer of spiritual books, within the walls of Olivet, he was known to us by his Trappist name, Brother Philip. Six months into my novitiate, I had never laid eyes on him. He was the only brother at Olivet to be granted permission to build a hermitage. One summer years earlier, he had constructed a small cabin up in the mountains behind the monastery. Even so, he was required to rejoin the community every year on St. Michael's Day. And each year, on St. Michael's eve, a fresh recruit was sent into the woods to retrieve him.

Later I discovered that his books took up an entire shelf in the monastery library. Among the thirty or so volumes of poetry, social criticism, monastic histories, and studies in contemplative spirituality, we had at least a dozen copies of his famous autobiography, each in a different language. Widely translated, it is often favorably compared to Augustine's *Confessions*. Just recently, Mason's original, handwritten manuscripts were donated to the special collections library at Columbia University, where he had studied as an undergraduate and served as editor of its literary magazine.

Had I known even these few details about him at the time, I might have made a better show of it. But then, I might've also embarrassed him with the kind of idolatrous fawning he despised. Outside the abbey he was Trevor Mason, literary celebrity; inside, he was Brother Philip, irascible prophet of the western Cascades.

I walked to the top of the first hill and stopped to get my bearings. It had been cold down in the shadow of the monastery, but up here the sun warmed me. Birds sang and squirrels chattered in the canopy. I held up my compass and aimed myself northeast, in the direction of the highest peak in the distance, the one Father Louis had pointed out.

As I recall now, the hike was not so difficult. Granted, thirty memory-softening years have intervened, but it was easier than most scout hikes, despite being uphill most of the way. I stopped a few times to nibble the bread and sip from the water bottle. The scenery was beautiful—mostly fir trees and ferns, awash in several gurgling streams, and of course the fresh, cool air of early autumn.

The map was easy to follow, with major landmarks clearly labeled and the relative space between them nearly always accurate. I was glad I had the compass, especially in the undergrowth, but much of the way I simply followed an old logging trail. Brother Timothy, poor soul, must've been in pretty awful shape to have gotten himself lost. For one thing, you can see down to the monastery from several openings along the path. Even without a compass you could find your way home in daylight. Timothy must've been a city boy through and through. Maybe it had been foggy the year before, and he got turned around somehow.

As I crested the final peak of the journey, I looked out over a ravine. According to the map, Brother Philip's hermitage was somewhere just ahead. I could see why he had chosen such a spot. Far as the eye could see was forested greenery. No hint of human occupation anywhere. The luscious hills crisscrossed one over the other in a landscape worthy of Thomas Cole or Asher Durand. For someone called to eremitic life, this was an ideal location. With a minimum of supplies, you could enjoy nature in all her glory, assuming you could hunt and forage—and live without the consolation of human company.

The map did not record elevations, only direction. By my reckoning, the X that marked the spot of Brother Philip's cabin was straight ahead. Which meant straight down, down into a steep ravine. I wondered if this were the spot where Brother Timothy had begun to doubt the map and double back, or maybe he turned aside along the ridge. After all, who could build a cabin on such a steep downslope? And why? I was still trying to justify poor Timothy, and maybe reinforce my own courage at the same time.

It was a classic dilemma: when asked to believe the unbelievable, most of us look for a reasonable alternative, a compromise that affirms the testimony of our senses and yet remains true to the spirit of the doctrine to which we cling. Well now. If I had rightly interpreted the "test," and if the Brother Timothy tale had been told as some sort of clue to guide me, then my path lay directly ahead—down what looked from the peak to be a nearly impassable cliff. To turn aside would be to surrender to doubt. To trust the Abbot's map and venture into peril, surely this was the right choice.

I held up the map to give some assurance. I checked the compass. These two things had done what they had been designed to do. Brother Bartholomew had taught us some Kierkegaard that summer. The tousled old Dane had said more than once that the leap of faith was the singular path to enlightenment. A literal leap at this point would've produced a spectacular tumble into the ravine. A more measured descent was required, but a descent nonetheless.

A memory from my brief scout days dropped into my mind. On one of our hikes, the troop leader had taught us to listen like deer. *Have you ever noticed*, he said, *how deer turn their stiff ears like antenna? They are focusing their hearing.* The guide taught us to cup our palms around the backside of our ears, fold them slightly forward, and slowly turn our heads. Sure enough, we could hear better. The sounds of the forest became focused and amplified by this simple directional trick.

I cupped my hands around my ears and slowly turned my head. Immediately the chatter of insects became more prominent. And various bird songs presented themselves from different levels of the canopy. From down in the ravine I heard the babble of rippling water. You would need a freshwater creek to live independently out here. This reinforced my trust in the map. I looked at the soles of my boots—good tread, barely worn. Had I been given these boots for the surefooted purpose of this descent? As a further act of faith, I finished the barley loaf and drained the remaining water. I would launch myself into the unknown without provision for the future. I would either meet Brother Philip somewhere down this steep mountainside, or I would end up like Brother Timothy, the brunt of an exemplary tale for next year's novice.

I whispered a brief prayer to St. Michael as I turned sideways and led with my left foot, allowing it to slide a bit in the dirt while my hand trailed and acted like a rudder in the dirt, sometimes grabbing a branch or root to slow my progress. It's surprisingly hard work going down such a steep decline. We use a different set of muscles than for a typical climb. Lose your grip in such conditions and you can easily tumble ass over teakettle until . . . ? Well, I suppose until you hit up against some outgrowth or other, tearing tendons and breaking bones on the way. I made slow progress down the hillside, going about two hundred yards before I spotted the tarpaper and rock roof of Brother Philip's modest cabin.

To avoid startling him, I made a megaphone with my hands and called out: "Halloooo! Brother Philip! Halloooo, there in the cabin!" No response. There were no windows or doors on the backside of the cabin; in fact, it looked like the cabin emerged from the hillside itself, the extension of a cave.

I saw a huge boulder jutting from the brush just below me. I scurried down to it, pulled my way up the side of the boulder, and stood atop it, waving my arms and calling: "Halloooo there in the cabin!"

I looked around for a rock to bounce off the roof. But before I could find one, I saw his bald head appear, and then the white robe and black scapular as he rounded the corner. His face turned upwards and he shaded his eyes with one hand. He pointed at me. "Don't move!" he shouted. He disappeared back around the corner briefly, then suddenly began climbing the hillside with the energy and agility of a mountain goat. In his right hand he held a long staff. As he made his way uphill, I realized it was not a staff, or not *just* a staff; it was topped by a blade! A long, curved scythe reflected the late afternoon sunlight. It jounced as Brother Philip climbed. For a time the scythe was the only thing visible, bobbling above the thick shrubbery, and then his bald head would appear again, then disappear just as quick, as Brother Philip made his way up the steep side of the ravine.

My first impulse was to run. A mad monk, wielding some sort of hand-crafted weapon, was coming for me! Despite his crazed behavior, I trusted his command. Kierkegaard again? If Brother Philip were to be my executioner, so be it. I had nothing to lose but my silly life. I confess my heart fluttered with adrenaline, but I stayed put. Anyway, I was not likely to outrun a man who had obviously been scaling this cliff for years. So I stood awkwardly perched on the boulder, awaiting the lunatic.

As he drew near, I saw that his face was flushed and he was laboring for breath. Yet on he charged, his eyes wild with purpose. Just shy of the big boulder, he raised the blade high and brought it down into the soil at the base of the giant granite rock. He raised it twice more, slicing down both times with the kind of fierceness once shown by medieval lancers. I remained frozen atop my rock. Finally, he leaned on the upright pole, dark red blood dripping down the scythe. He stood there until his breath slowed. I remained silent.

I peeked over the edge of the boulder. There in the dirt lay a dismembered rattlesnake. It's head and tail had been sliced cleanly off. Eerily, its midsection continued to wriggle for a moment before Brother Philip picked it up. "I'm sorry, snake. I honor your presence with me here on the mountainside, and I regret the necessity to take your life." He held it aloft and intoned, "Heavenly Father, I thank you for the friendship of this creature. Please forgive me for killing it. May its flesh nourish our bodies. We receive this bounty as from your loving hands. Amen." Looking down at the base of the rock, he spoke to me now, "Its nest was here, at the base of this granite, you see. Watch your step. It had many children."

He turned and began to walk/slide back down to his cabin. Over his shoulder he instructed, "Bury its head and bring the tail with you." He scurried down the cliffside. From atop the boulder it looked like he was riding a skateboard. I slid down off the big boulder and dug with my hands a small trench beneath the edge of the rock. I covered the snake's head and tamped down the dirt with my boot. I picked up the rattle and counted fourteen segments. Following Brother Philip's method, I leaned my body into the slope, and let my feet slide down the cliffside to the edge of his wooden deck.

Around the front of the cabin, he stood in the center of the deck, stripped to his skivvies. He motioned for me to sit in the only chair, a rough-hewn Adirondack. His torso and legs were lean and muscled but his skin was exceedingly pale and smooth. Only his face and neck were tanned and heavily wrinkled. I thought at that moment that he resembled a tortoise who had shed its shell. Before I knew what was happening, he had lugged a bucket of soapy water and a large bristle brush in front of the chair. He unlaced my boots, yanked them off, and beat the dust from them. He peeled my sweaty socks from my feet and laid them out over the railing to dry.

Although I was deeply embarrassed by the enactment of this tender ritual, I understood it to be an expression of our Benedictine piety, in which every visitor must be greeted as Christ. Ordinarily the washing of feet was a Holy Week activity, practiced in the monastery as part of our Maundy Thursday liturgy. The symbolism was crucial to our Cistercian identity. But out here in the woods, it had an intensely practical value: my feet were indeed dirty, and very sore. The borrowed hiking boots were a size too small for me. My feet were blistered and blotched and caked with soil and sweat.

Brother Philip dunked each foot in the bucket, then plopped it on the towel across his lap and brushed it down like a shoe-shine boy doing the final buff and polish on a pair of loafers. I looked down at his liver-spotted scalp while he worked. He whistled the old Cole Porter song, "Just One of Those Things." He looked surprised that I knew the tune.

"You're a strange bird, aren't you?" he said. "What are the odds that a young monk like you would know your Cole Porter?"

"About the same," I said, "as the odds that a hermit deep in the Oregon wild would be found whistling tunes from the American songbook."

He smiled, revealing a tangle of darkened teeth. "My mother took me to see *Jubilee* when I was a lad. The big hit in that show was 'Begin the Beguine,' but I never liked that song."

When he had cleaned my feet better than I ever have, he toweled them dry and massaged them with oil. He laid the towel over the railing, next to my socks, and emptied the bucket into the ravine. I heard the water splash against the rocks, some distance below the deck. All this time I sat there holding the snake's rattle. He plucked it from my hand. Taking a nail and hammer from a footlocker, he tacked the rattle to the edge of the roof, next to several others—all hanging in a row.

THE CABIN STANDS to this day. The monks of Olivet allow small groups to hold retreats in it during spring and fall. And of course it is a place of pilgrimage now for those who pursue Brother Philip's case for sainthood. Only last winter I was interviewed by the Vatican official in charge of his beatification. Although Brother Philip's radical pacifism is not embraced by the conservative church hierarchy, there has nevertheless been a consistent and compelling case for his canonization since the very day of his death, which came about three months after that Michaelmas night we spent together on the deck of his cabin.

I returned once, a few weeks later, and then only in broad daylight.

It is an extraordinary place. The small cabin clings to the side of the mountain, with an amazing view of the Cascade wilderness stretching easterly as far as the eye can see. Brother Philip had anchored the cabin to the granite shelf and built its one room into an existing shallow cave. It was a modest yet comfortable place. The cistern on the roof captured more rainwater than he could use, and a flagstone path led to an outhouse just twenty steps off the deck. Brother Philip and I spent most of our time together that night on his rustic wooden deck, which hung out over the forest below at a treacherous angle.

It was only a week past the equinox. As we sat silently and watched the afternoon turn to evening, the sun dropped beneath the ridgeline behind us, causing the wilderness laid out before us to fill with shadows. The air cooled quickly; soon my naked feet grew cold, so I pulled back on my damp woolen socks. Brother Philip put on his cassock, slipped a knit cap over his bald head, and made us a pot of tea. The sky darkened all around us as the old monk made evening preparations.

He disappeared around the other corner of his deck and reemerged with an armload of firewood. In no time he built a small but steady fire in an iron pot that sat on the far corner of the deck. As he cooked the rattlesnake over it, I silently watched the stars brighten in the vivid nighttime sky. I have never experienced a night sky like that again. It was as if we had been lifted up into space and all the features of the Milky Way were our near neighbors. My experience of the night sky has been muted ever since by the ambient light of one city or another. That night on Brother Philip's deck is the only time in my life that the word *cosmos* had palpable meaning.

The rattlesnake meat was sweet and tender. Brother Philip roasted some wild mushrooms in herbs to go with it. After dinner he carried a jug from the darkness of his cabin and offered me some. "Take a big gulp," he said, "then guess what it is." I followed his direction, nearly spewing the thick brew. "It tastes like cider, only sweeter." I took another swallow. "It's a little spicy," I added.

"Mead," he proclaimed. "There's a hive down by the creek. With a little smoke to soothe them, the bees are very willing to share. Mix the honey with a little water and wine yeast. And from then on it's out of your hands. The maturation comes only with time. And of course time, timing, is everything." He said that without pretense; however, even as the sentence passed his lips I had the feeling that he was speaking of more than just fermentation.

He brought out a bowl of blackberries for dessert. We sat on the deck, now warmly zipped into sleeping bags, me propped at a heavenly viewing angle in the old Adirondack chair, our stomachs full, our senses alert. "Do you know this Michaelmas legend? When St. Michael threw Satan out of heaven, he fell to earth and was caught among thorns in a blackberry bramble. Sure enough, any berries left on the bush after September are too bitter to eat. Only the rats will take them then."

I slowly drained my jar of mead. Sparks drifted up into the cool air as the fire gradually reduced to embers. When the firelight in the iron pot grew pale, the fire of the stars surrounding us blazed seemingly within reach. The cicadas were particularly loud, clicking and chirping and buzzing, a last gasp of summer hullaballoo as autumn moved in.

In the distance a coyote howled and two more answered him with barks. Another noisy creature lumbered through the trees beneath us, rustling and snapping branches as it moved. Perhaps noting my nervousness, Brother Philip said, "Don't worry. Most of these creatures are friendly. Some are curious and sniff about the cabin at night, but they rarely come on to the deck." It was the indeterminate nature of that word *rarely* that kept me a little on edge.

"I did have one visitor that surprised me. I sleep indoors during the winter months. And this was back in, oh, late February, maybe early March. I don't have a calendar. Anyway, it had snowed most of the day, so the night was particularly bright, with the moon reflecting off the trees and the deck—like a pale blue spotlight. Understand, I don't get visitors. I'm too far from the state park for even the most lost of hikers. The fire-watchers check in with me during the summer months. But the winter out here passes in darkness and in silence, and my solitude goes on and ever on.

"This visitor wore clothes that looked brand new. And even though my thermometer said 30 degrees, you couldn't see his breath. I did not hear his steps. In fact, I didn't hear him at all. I had just finished my Compline prayers and stood to extinguish the lamp. I caught a glimpse of him out of the corner of my eye, through my only window, there—the figure of a man gazing out at the night as we are now. He wasn't looking in; he was gazing out.

"When I opened the window, he wasn't startled. He smiled. 'Aren't you going to offer me some tea?' he said in French. He called me Trevor, and he spoke with the same accent as my father, who came from a small village near Provence. Suddenly my childhood language returned to me. I hadn't spoken French in fifty years. 'Are you lost?' I asked him. He shook his head. I came out here and lit the fire, which took some doing since the fire pot was filled with fresh powder. I told him, 'Wait inside if you like. It's a bit warmer in there.' 'I prefer the deck,' he said.

"We passed the time waiting for the kettle to boil in silence. I know that sounds odd—that I wouldn't think to engage him in further talk. But you see for most of the year I live deliberately in the absence of words. And during winter especially it simply doesn't occur to me to speak. It seems . . . I don't know, unnatural. My words sound ugly compared with the eloquence of deep silence. The woods were silent that night, too—not like tonight. Why, I've used more words with you today than I have in months. We marveled together, the stranger and I, at the brightness and the whiteness all around.

"When I handed him his tea, he removed his knit cap. In the moonlight I could see his long hair flowing down past his shoulders. I've never seen such hair before. Between that and the accent, he gave the impression of a man out of time. As though he had stepped out of another age, maybe the past, maybe the future, I can't say. His face was younger than his voice. We stood sipping our tea and looking out over the glistening treetops. The stars weren't nearly as prominent as they are tonight. And the air around us seemed to warm, a dangerous illusion. You've perhaps heard of freezing men who believed they were burning up with fever? Even so, I offered him my warm jacket, which he refused. He didn't appear to be cold at all.

"Finally I asked him, 'Why have you come?' 'I've come to offer three visions,' he said. 'Are you ready to receive them?' 'Yes,' I answered. 'Close your eyes,' he said. I closed them, and immediately my skin began to tingle all over, not because I was afraid—I was at peace—but my nerves were, how shall I say it, enlivened. And in a moment I experienced my life as I might have lived it outside the monastery. It was a lifetime of memories, as if I had actually lived each moment of it, but it arrived in my consciousness in a flash. It was a good life, a meaningful one in which I enjoyed the pleasures of a family and the success of the New York literary community, whose attention I craved before my conversion. I wrote novels, fathered children, traveled the world and enjoyed its pleasures. I experienced the pain of loss, the death of a wife, and the renewal of love upon marrying a second time. I suffered numerous character faults, but none of them overtook me. And in the end I died a peaceful death surrounded by my second wife, children, and grandchildren. I was mourned throughout the world. Then I opened my eyes."

"Extraordinary. So you saw what your life might have been if you had not taken the vows?"

"It was more than just seeing it. I felt it. I lived it in this very body. All of the pains and pleasures of that life were as vivid as real memories. And then, before I could think further, the visitor asked me to close my eyes again. I felt a warm sensation within. This warming began in my stomach and spread throughout my body. It rose into my chest and throat and scalp. Just as before, I experienced another lifetime in a flash, an instant. It was the nearest I have come to understanding eternity. The veil of time as we experience it was lifted. It was my own life I saw, just as I have lived it, but I was not living it in my body, but in the bodies of those who felt the effects of my prayers.

"One of the great temptations of the monk's life—if you've not felt this yet you soon will—is the doubt that your prayers are truly efficacious, that is, that they move beyond the boundaries of your own soul and achieve some actual good in the world. But the mystery of the Holy Spirit is vast and deep. Our prayers extend far beyond what we can imagine. And in this vision I saw others, those I have never met, never knew existed, healed from malady, reconciled to enemies, comforted in distress. I was given to see the effects of my own devotion beyond the bounds of my awareness. The warming subsided. Again I opened my eyes."

The old monk had tears running down his cheeks as he told me this.

"The strange thing is I felt no pride in this. I did not make this strange world, after all, I'm just a very small being in a very large universe. I realized these visions were answers to my own prayers about the doubts and fears that have haunted me ever since I came to this retreat. Instead of praying all day, I should be feeding the poor, caring for the sick—doing the acts of mercy instead of praying for them. But this vision brought me peace through the understanding that my life would have achieved purpose almost regardless of my choices. We are intricately connected, you see, in ways we cannot imagine. And God's mercy will not be impeded."

He turned to me. "Your life, whether in Olivet or somewhere else, will flower with God's purpose, monk or layman. Most of what you achieve you will never know. It's better that way. The ego is a con man, you see, from start to finish, and he must be denied his self-aggrandizing project in favor of divine purpose. He must be driven into a cave and starved."

I wasn't sure what this meant, but I nodded as if I did. "And the third vision?"

He turned to gaze at the forest again. "A third time the visitor asked me to close my eyes. And this time I was overtaken by a chill. My body cooled from head to toe. All was darkness. And then I realized that behind my eyelids I was looking into the night sky. It was *this* view, the one we now share, but there was no cabin and there were no trees and the stars were dim. All was silence. The full moon appeared, and then a second moon, and a third. 'Count the moons,' my visitor said. 'You have as many moons as appear in your sky left in this life,' and then, 'Trevor, you will be received into the everlasting joy of your savior.' A fourth, fifth, and sixth moon appeared—all right in a row. And then another and another and another. Nine moons in all. I waited for more, but they did not arise."

Brother Philip pointed at the moon that now hung over the treetops. "That is the sixth moon."

When he said this I felt a chill throughout my body, even though I was zipped into a warm sleeping bag. It took me a moment to process this— that he had been given a deadline, of sorts, on his very life. I wanted to console him at the prospect of his impending death. But he was not distressed. "I'm sorry," I said.

"Then you believe the vision?"

"Perhaps there is some symbolic message," I answered.

"Poppycock. Of course it's symbolism. Who says symbols are not real? And there are worse things than death, young man." He began to sing . . . "Be like the bluebird who never is blue" . . . a rollicking song about a wise bluebird who saw clearly his own folly and yet remained joyful, a bird who sang through his troubles—not as a means of escape but rather as a path to transcendence.

"Cole Porter again?" I asked.

"Not his best number, but one that sticks in the brain," he said. "When I opened my eyes my visitor was gone. He left behind this knit cap lying in the snow. Best hat I ever had. He left no footprints."

"Was it St. Michael?"

"I think perhaps archangels have better things to do than magic tricks on wooden decks in the middle of the night. At least I hope so. But an angel, surely, since he overcame my fears and doubts and brought me peace and consolation. And such is the work of angels. When we hike out of here tomorrow, it will be for the last time. Farewell, sweet solitude."

I felt the exhaustion of my day overtake me. It had been months since I had stepped outside the monastery; the hike and the mead and the cool nighttime air conspired to draw me into slumber. I closed my eyes and leaned my head against the tall chair back, hoping that no visitor and no vision would intrude upon my rest. Two or three times during the night I awoke briefly and saw Brother Philip seated in meditation on the edge of the deck, his back to me, covered in his sleeping bag, his head topped by the angel's knit cap. He kept vigil through the final night of his hermitage, like a seated Buddha, silhouetted against the bright stars and the gibbous moon.

I awoke to the sun shining directly on my face as it rose above the distant rim of the western Cascades, eliminating the shadows of the forest and evaporating the dew that covered Brother Philip's little deck. I took a moment to appreciate the time and the place before I unzipped the sleeping bag and stumbled to the outhouse.

When I returned, Brother Philip was gone. He had hiked one final time down to the creek to bid farewell to the bees and the trout and the little herb and vegetable garden that had nourished him for so many years. Standing on the deck, the sun shone brightly into Brother Philip's cabin, completely lighting the interior, which had only been a dark chasm to me the night before.

Now, as I walked through his open door, I saw on the back wall a mural that he had painted. It was a large rendering of the resurrection. At some point during his long hermitage, Brother Philip had gotten someone to bring him some paints and brushes. He had painted a somewhat elemental rocky cave opening that arched completely across the plastered back wall of the cabin, perhaps a rendering of the very cave in which he had anchored this cabin so long ago, the cave in which I now stood. And inside the tomb opening, he had painted a luminous light, the sort of golden light that animates the divine in all the classic icons of our faith. And deep inside the tomb, for he had enough artistic skill to replicate the perspective of depth, was a rock-hewn burial bench. And on the bench lay the famous shroud, wrinkled and discarded, draped over the granite. He who had been dead was alive again, and the golden light depicted the afterglow of the great transformation. Brother Philip's bunk lay just beneath the shroud. He had slept here in the tomb for decades. I stood transfixed. Even though the painting lacked the spit and polish of a professional mural, clearly it had been executed by a man who had lived in the presence of such divine light and basked in its sacred warmth.

Brother Philip's silhouette filled the doorway, blocking the dawn's light. "Amateur work," he said casually, ducking inside the doorway, "but I had to do something to brighten the place up." He took a rucksack off a hook near the door and began to pack. "The wisdom of the tortoise," he said, "is that he carries everything he needs in life on his back. Such is the great advantage of poverty."

In a few minutes he stood again in the doorway and glanced around the room one last time. In a corner was a waist-high stack of journals. In a few weeks Father Louis would send me back to the cabin with two other monks to pack those out and store them in a locked cabinet in the library. Only the designee of his New York publisher would have access to the remaining books that lay yet unedited within those journals. (As I write this, all of his writings have now seen the light of publication.) One of the monks would bring a camera on our trek to take a photographic record of the cabin as he had left it. All of this happened without Brother Philip's knowledge or consent since he was occupied with the bone cancer that would take him from us faster than anyone thought. Anyone, that is, but he and I, since I was the only person he told about the nighttime visitor.

I WRITE THIS now, at the request of Father Louis' successor, upon the thirtieth anniversary of Brother Philip's death. The monks are collecting all living memories for a special archive of his life at Olivet, with the added benefit to the advocates for Brother Philip's canonization who will use the records in support of their cause.

On that final morning, as we closed up his cabin, Brother Philip locked the door and tossed the key as far as he could into the ravine. I took note of its trajectory and had very little trouble relocating the key among the fir needles when I returned.

I had difficulty keeping up with Brother Philip that morning. Even though he had not slept the night before and I had, my legs ached from the previous day's hike and my feet were sore inside the borrowed hiking boots. He huffed and puffed like a small diesel engine but his pace never varied. Surefooted and agile, he climbed and hiked like a man half his age. Well, I'm laughing now as I write this because at the time I was less than half his age and I stopped three times on the way back to lean against a tree trunk, catch my breath, and rub my aching calves.

It was the second Sunday in Advent when he died. The doctor had made his final visit two days prior, and he had warned us that it would not be much longer. He increased Brother Philip's morphine dosage and gave final instructions to Brother John, who had completed two years at Harvard Medical before taking the vows. John was at his side when he passed, as was Father Louis, who has also since passed on.

Father Louis wrote the narrative of Brother Philip's death, since it marked the first of the miracles now attributed to him. Just as Brother Philip breathed his last, another monk lying near him in the infirmary, Brother Andrew, who had broken his back while chopping down a dead sycamore, was completely healed and stood from his bed, saying that Brother Philip had come to him in his delirium and explained that with his death Andrew would be restored. But I will entrust you to Brother Louis's narrative for that story. At least six other miracles have been recorded in Brother Philip's name, four more than are required by the Vatican to verify a candidate's suitability for sainthood. It is only the liberal nature of Brother Philip's social criticism that has slowed the process.

I have no personal stake in his candidacy, but I am more than willing to share my unique experience since it gives me a chance to share the inspiration I received from knowing him only a few brief months. I left the monastery upon the occasion of my one-year anniversary at Olivet. I did so in great confidence because of something Brother Philip said to me that night on the deck of his cabin when he intimated that my vocation might lay outside the walls of Olivet. In fact, I consider my work here in Chicago as a psychotherapist my true vocation, and my year at Olivet as the all-important first step in my journey.

Brother Philip's comments about the disingenuous nature of the ego stuck with me and prompted further study and practice. I have since studied all of Brother Philips's books and consider him my primary mentor. His books on contemplative practice elucidated his theory that the ego constitutes a "false self" that must be transcended and superseded by the "true self," the divine personality that can only be cultivated in humility and poverty of spirit—the very soil of the monastic garden.

I took the spiritual work that Brother Philip taught in contemplative prayer and used it as my root therapeutic principle. In thirty years of teaching, counseling, and writing, I find myself still quoting Brother Philip and still ruminating on the story of his angelic visit. I have told and retold that story to my patients and students as a parable of human vocation.

Of course, I had no inkling whatsoever of this when I met that strange, lovable old monk, who slew a serpent on the side of a mountain and graciously cooked it over an open fire, nourishing me in body, mind, and spirit, and offering inspiration for a career, indeed a life. When Brother Bartholomew launched me through the back gate of the monastery garden that morning thirty years ago, I thought that I had either been exiled or sent on a mission. In fact, it was both. My whole life pivoted that night beneath the stars. The experience marked my final days as a monk and signaled a way of being in the world that I had previously been unable to imagine. More, I was given a glimpse into eternal mysteries that have shaped my thoughts ever since. Whoever you are, whatever your circumstance as you read this, may your life also flourish in the golden light of the resurrection.

NOTHING ON MY TONGUE
BUT HALLELUJAH

Love is not a victory march.
—*Leonard Cohen*

IF I WERE CAPABLE OF HUMAN EMOTIONS, MY RESPONSE TO the death of Margaret and Stanley would be overwhelming sadness. How I yearn to feel as they felt. Alas and alack. Mortals in the not so distant past used to utter that phrase to express sorrow, regret, dismay. I can feel none of those things, yet somehow, when I consider their fate, this small package of human verbiage seems to convey the appropriate response. Alas and alack. We angels might also just as well exclaim hosanna and hallelujah, a verbal package we are known for in some human circles.

Stanley was the name of my initial charge during that period of time humans call the early twenty-first century. But Stanley's fate had become so intermingled with Margaret's that I also took Margaret under my watch. The mechanics of the assignment are less germane to my testimony than the circumstances. I bear witness to the final morning of their lives as an emblem of the manner in which the innocent are so often called to suffer.

Margaret had passed another restless night of dreams and fitful awakenings. She was used to it by now and endured it with such equanimity that few besides her husband knew of her nightly travails. This morning she scooped the coffee beans into the grinder and pushed the button. When Stanley heard the machine's loud whine above the sound of Chopin's Nocturnes, he shuffled into the kitchen, getting the mugs down from the shelf and the milk from the refrigerator. His hip was aching today but not as bad as some days. As the coffee percolated, he stood next to Margaret at the kitchen window that looked out at the creek and the mountain beyond.

They had seen that sky before, twenty years earlier, during the Jensen fire in September of 1998. But the rain had come to the rescue then, allowing the Cal Fire teams to gain the upper hand. This fire now was coming fast and hot out of the northwest, fueled by high winds and preceded by a five-year drought. Today there was no rain in the forecast, even though it was November and rain was overdue. The soupy blend of dark gray was tinged by a reddish underglow. Darkness loomed over the mountaintop, while heavy smoke made breathing more difficult with each passing hour.

"It's beautiful, isn't it?" Margaret said.

"It is, sort of."

"If you can detach yourself from what it means for us. If you can just hover like an angel and gaze upon it dispassionately. If you can view it with God's eyes."

Stanley put his arm around his wife's shoulders. "I can't pretend to be God. Even so, I can appreciate it for its own strangeness."

"Think of it as a painting," Margaret said. "Like a mad sort of Hudson River piece."

"Like maybe Thomas Cole in an apocalyptic mood," Stanley added.

Margaret slid her arm around her husband's waist. "There's nobody I'd rather look upon this with but you."

"We've had an enormous run of luck, haven't we?"

"Grace upon grace." She let her hand take hold of his left buttock. "How's that damned prostate gland treating you this morning?"

"If I believed as you do in the supernatural, I'd say it's nearly time to call in the exorcist."

When the coffee pot announced its readiness with a series of electronic beeps, they took their places at the kitchen table. Stanley tucked his long legs beneath the table and adjusted in his seat to remove the pressure from his bad hip. Despite an intense round of initial treatment, the cancer had spread from his prostate to his bones. His head of wild Einstein hair had thinned out in response to chemotherapy; still it looked like a nest of sprung silver wires, no matter if he ran a brush through it or not. Were I capable of pure endearment, this trait alone would yield my affection,

"You must've had another of your prophetic dreams this morning," Stanley said, filling their mugs. "You were up early again."

"Did I wake you?" she asked.

"Not fully. I felt a disturbance in the Force is all. Even we mere mortals can sense it when a Jedi leaves the room."

Margaret stirred some milk and sweetener into her coffee. A short, heavy woman, she had a long mane of salt and pepper hair, which she twisted and clipped atop her head, emphasizing the roundness of her cheeks and the startling green of her eyes, the cheeks and once jet-black hair a trait inherited from her Wintu mother, and the eyes so many had described as soulful from her Scotch-Irish father.

"You know it's weird we still have power," she remarked. "The radio said power was out in the whole county. Yet here we are with our lights and coffee, our music and running water."

"The perks of living with a Jedi," Stanley said, toasting her with his mug. He took a long, slow draw of coffee. He held the mug beneath his nose and breathed in its steam. "I'm going to miss the smell of coffee," he said. "I'm going to miss this morning ritual with you, my love. Forty-four years of this. I've grown accustomed."

"Whatever heaven is like, there must be an eternal equivalent to this," Margaret mused. "'More than we could ask or imagine,' scripture says. That's what God has in store for us."

"I'll settle for the memory, whatever form I take next. If ashes remember, I'll remember. If by some miracle we do retain consciousness, or whatever the ashy equivalent of consciousness, I'll settle for the sweetness of memory."

"Listen to that," Margaret said, cocking her head to the music. "This is my favorite one. In this one Chopin achieves a perfect mixture of joy and melancholy."

There was no way for Margaret to know that Frederic Chopin had also been in my charge. Mortals often remark on the world's seeming smallness; if they only knew the intricate complexity of the temporal and spatial web in which they exist. From the angelic perspective, Margaret might have reached out her hand and laid it upon the tousled head of Chopin seated at his instrument. I have full recall of the stormy morning Chopin composed that piece. Like Margaret, he had slept fitfully the night before. The storm's ionic charge invigorated his spirit, and the melody flowed through his fingers like fresh water through a spring.

Margaret continued, "It's all about the balance between the left hand and the right hand. Can you hear it?"

"I wish you still played for me," Stanley said.

"I cannot compete with Madame Engerer," Margaret said. "And it's no fun when your fingers no longer respond to the signals your brain is sending them."

They listened together. After Margaret's favorite nocturne ended and the next one began, Stanley said, "I'm ready for my morning dream report."

"All right. This one was disturbing but also curiously comforting. We were young again," Margaret began, "as we are in so many of these dreams. And we lived somewhere else, in another time and place. We had children, a boy and a girl. The boy was about ten, and the girl was younger, maybe three, and nothing like our Catherine. She was a tiny thing, with a ponytail atop her head and a frilly little dress. Not at all our gangly tomboy Catherine. She was holding your hand.

"As I recall," she continued, "we were walking in a procession, toward a glass temple. Our little boy had run ahead to join some of his friends. And the three of us—you and the girl and me—were walking together in a large procession. I was carrying a tray of some sort. An offering. Don't ask me how I know that. You know how you know things in dreams sometimes? We were to participate in some sort of ritual instituted by a relatively new government. There was a history there, though I can't say what it was exactly. There had been a long tradition of a republic, I believe, and now this place, in this time, had chosen a dictator, or an emperor. And this procession was a part of a new rite. Isn't it strange how thorough a dream world can seem?"

"I know that feeling. Some dreams come complete with their own backstory."

"Yes, and the backstory is just taken for granted, the way some people in our dreams are definitely people from our waking lives, even though they may look or act nothing like them. Anyway, we were all a community of shared values. We were all wearing the same kind of clothing. Something like robes or togas. Yes, we were all in white togas, and we were walking in procession toward this glass temple. And the women were balancing these trays. I myself held a tray with four small animal sacrifices. They must have been doves. For some reason I think they were doves." Margaret reached across the table. "Take my hand," she said to Stanley.

"You're shaking," he said.

"It's because I'm still clinging to that dream. It still seems a little more real than just a dream. Some of them feel like alternate lives. Like I've lived another life in that other world, and then reawakened into this life. But that other life keeps hold for a while. The feeling wears off with time, but for a little while it stays vivid, until it's replaced with activity in this life, the waking life. I need to feel your grip to reinforce the reality of this life."

He took her hand between both of his hands.

"So we were all in this procession, walking. Everybody knew one another. These were our neighbors. The women were all carrying trays like mine. On the trays we carried our sacrifices. Then, out of the corner of my eye, I saw this young man emerge from the woods. He was a monk—you know, wearing a brown frock like certain monks wear. And he was carrying a pitcher. In the church we call it a flagon. You know the flagon that holds the communion wine? Like that. And the fluid inside the flagon was sloshing out, spilling on his robe and on the path. He made his way into the center of the processional, and people had to maneuver around him, the way water in the creek creates an eddy as it flows around a boulder.

"And then the monk sat down, right in the middle of the crowd. He sat and crossed his legs, the way they do when monks meditate. And he made eye contact with me. He was a young man, like all of us in the dream; we were all so young. Everybody in the processional was young and beautiful. No one was old or crippled or poor. So anyway, he sat down and, looking right at me, he emptied the flagon over his head. The liquid poured down his face, saturating his beard and darkening his frock. Then he struck a match. And he went up in flames."

"Holy shit."

"The flames engulfed him. They burned the whiskers off his face, making him appear even younger. The frock just exploded in flames. He didn't cry out. He looked totally calm. But I could see the anguish in his eyes as he burned. And then he toppled over. And still he burned."

"Ho-ly shit."

"I don't remember ever having the sense of smell in a dream before. But my nostrils filled with the stench of burning flesh. The people just walked around him. They watched him. They avoided the flames, like they were an inconvenience. They obviously saw all that we saw. Yet their reaction didn't fit the situation. They were not horrified. They went on with the processional. They continued carrying their sacrifices to the temple."

ALAS AND ALACK, just a few moments later Margaret and Stanley heard the thumpity-thump of a vehicle crossing the creek on the old wooden bridge. They exchanged a puzzled look. The public evacuation order had been given twenty-four hours earlier. For the first twelve hours they had heard the distant hum of traffic out on the main road. But this morning had been silent, save the present whine of what sounded now like a truck downshifting as it made its way up their driveway.

Margaret stood and peeked out the corner of the kitchen window. "Fire truck," she said.

"Duck down," Stanley said.

"Too late. He saw me." Margaret squinted. "I believe that's Charlie."

"Shit."

"Yes. It's Charlie. He's got that big walrus mustache. Very distinctive. We should've moved the car around back. He must've seen it sitting in the driveway."

"I guess the jig is up," said Stanley. "Shitty-shit-shit."

Margaret turned to face Stanley. "You're my Clyde Barrow," she said.

"And you're my Bonnie Parker."

"Are you ready for that hail of bullets?"

"I doubt if we'll feel much beyond the first dozen or so."

"I just hope he shoots straight."

The doorbell rang. Margaret answered. "Good morning, Charlie," she said, holding open the door. "I'll bet you've been busy."

"Yes, ma'am."

"You look tired, Charlie. Come on in . . . " She left the front door standing open and walked back into the kitchen. She glanced at Stanley with a look that said, *Let's not lose our resolve.*

"I can't stay . . . and neither can you," Charles said, stepping inside and closing the door behind him.

"I'll pour you a cup," Margaret said. She filled a mug for him and pulled out a third chair at the kitchen table.

"Mr. Reynolds," Charles said.

"Charles," Stanley said, nodding.

"You still have power?" Charles asked.

"Yes, how about that?" Margaret said.

"Hmm. You on a generator?" he asked.

"We have a Generac unit out back, but it hasn't kicked in since that big snowstorm last February," Stanley replied. "I believe it's out of fuel."

"I don't understand it. There is no power. The plant closed last night. They're all evacuated. But I guess you're right—I don't hear the motor."

"I imagine you worked all through the night," Margaret said.

"Yes, ma'am. This is my final sweep. The fire's just on the other side of the ridge. Once it tops the ridgeline, it'll be too late. Now is the time to leave. Actually, yesterday was the time to leave."

"Charlie, how's your sister doing?" Margaret asked.

"She's just fine, Mrs. Reynolds. The second round of chemo seems to have knocked the tumors back. Her last scan showed them to be just itty-bitty things. Thanks for asking."

"I'm so glad to hear that. Father Tim has included her in the prayers ever since the diagnosis. You might just call the church office and let Jenny know so she can update the bulletin."

"You do realize that the church won't survive."

"Oh . . . of course. I hadn't stopped to consider that. And I suppose the elementary school is also in the path of destruction."

"Frankly, nothing is expected to survive. This time tomorrow it'll all be gone. This town will look like the surface of the moon." He turned to Stanley. "Mr. Reynolds, are you having trouble getting your car started?"

"No."

"Because if your car's not working, you can ride out in my truck. I'm going all the way down to the evacuation center. We can even fit some of your paintings in the back. I'll cover them with a tarp."

Stanley was a painter and sculptor. Much of his late work was indeed destroyed in the fire; however, his reputation among mortals steadily rose in the decades following his death. Emile Bernard, one of his artistic role models, had also been in my charge—another "coincidence," as some choose to call them, of the elaborate web of interconnectivity. I do not have the verbal skill to even begin to explain the cosmic mingling of all creation. Is it enough to call it mind-boggling, another favorite expression of mortals in bygone days? *It simply boggles the mind* many of the best minds have said. *Hallelujah* is what we angels say.

"And I can call Cathy for you when we get there—"

"No, thank you, Charles," Stanley said. "We'll be just fine on our own."

"Mrs. Reynolds," Charles said, turning to Margaret, "you have to leave now. Do you understand? Nobody's seen winds like these. The fire is generating its own weather system. Once the flames top that ridge—"

"I'm so proud of you, Charlie," Margaret said. "So many of my students have become such accomplished men and women. You can't know how gratifying that is for me. Especially now that the world's grown so sour, so selfish and mean-spirited. To know that for forty years my first-graders were launched into their lives with kindness and with dignity, well, that's everything, you see. You can't imagine how proud I am of you all."

"We had a great teacher," Charles responded.

"I was there to give you a good start, that's all. You did the rest."

"Mr. and Mrs. Reynolds, you have to get into my truck now. You don't want to stay any longer. This fire is a new kind of monster. We've never seen the likes of this. Please. I'm begging you. Let me call Cathy. I'll have her meet us down at the shelter."

"Catherine's got a lot on her plate right now. We'll be fine on our own, Charles," Stanley said firmly. "Don't you give us another thought."

"Please, Mr. Reynolds. Mrs. Reynolds. You don't want to stay. It's not a good way to go. It's really not what you want. I know it's not what Cathy wants. For God's sake, please just get in your car now and follow me down. Or I can fit you into my truck. The cab is plenty big for all three of us. We can put some small bags in your lap, if you like, essentials . . . "

"It's so kind of you to stop, Charlie. Thank you for that. But this world that you're going down into, it's like foreign and hostile territory to us. The world simply isn't the one we ever imagined living in. It's not at all the world we wanted to help create when we were young. It's turned so cold, you see. It's not at all hospitable to people like us. You're young enough to endure it. Maybe you even have enough energy to see some changes come. But this world as it is . . . with the trajectory it's on . . . " Margaret shrugged her shoulders and gently shook her head.

"Charles, do you remember the Wintu family that lived in the farmhouse just down the creek from us?" Stanley asked. "Big family. A dozen kids or more."

"No, sir."

"I guess you wouldn't. I'm going way back in memory now. But maybe you remember that old boarded up house that stood down there where the Shell station is now? Back when you were in Margie's class you would've walked past it on your way to school."

"I think so. That's going back a ways."

"Well, the Wintu tribe once lived all over these mountains. They were forest people. Probably you learned something about them in Margie's class. And the old grandfather in that house used to tell a story about a great fire that swept through here ages ago, like Noah's flood, only fire not water. The Wintu saw fire as purgation, you see, as a way for the earth to cleanse herself. He said his ancestors alone survived it because their dwelling was covered in pinesap that had been drawn for them by a sympathetic woodpecker. The great fire burned everything in its path but passed over their little mud house. They alone survived, huddled together inside this mud hut covered with this special sap."

Margaret and Stanley had already, in their imaginations, begun to shuffle off this mortal coil, you see. Even before the fire's first spark, they had begun to anticipate the end of their pilgrimage. Charles, however, found such imaginings unthinkable. For him the sin of despair was an unacceptable flaw. Alas, he was not quite as smart as these two elders; he only half-listened to Stanley's story because he was trying, in his sleepy, overworked brain, to devise a plan to manipulate them into his truck. Mentioning their only daughter Catherine, a childhood friend and schoolmate of Charles's, was his trump card. He had already played it, and now he felt stumped by its failure.

Stanley continued: "When the fire had passed and it was safe for the Wintu family to come outside, a red-tailed hawk lit on the roof and cried out that it was time to live again. They were to repopulate the forest. But before he flew away, the hawk warned that if they didn't care for the land properly, the fire would return for them. And he had a little trick he would do, this old granddad, whenever he would tell this story. He would stick a pine branch into the fireplace and light it up like a torch. And he would hold the branch up, like this, and right when he said that someday the fire would return, the flame on the torch would flare up—he had put some kerosene on the wood, you see, and just at the right moment it would go *whoosh!* like that," Stanley said, smiling. "That branch would flare up. 'So be good to the earth, children,' he would say, 'or the mother who nurtures you will become an angry grizzly and devour us all.' You can imagine how big the eyes of the children in the room would grow."

"Mr. Reynolds. Your house will not be spared."

"Oh, Charles. I believe you may have missed my meaning. No matter. Your mug is nearly empty, son. I imagine you've got a schedule to keep."

Charles took a bandanna from around his neck and went to the sink. He soaked the bandanna in cold water and wiped his forehead and face with it. He cocked his head, listening to the music. "I remember this," he said.

"Chopin," Margaret said.

He nodded and wrapped the bandanna around his neck again. "I never could get this piece right," he said. "I could play the right hand but not the left. You were so patient with me. But I was a lousy piano student."

"It was not your gift," she said.

"No, ma'am. It was yours though. You played it for me, played it all the way through one afternoon to show me how it should sound. I remember thinking as I was listening that it was the most beautiful music I had ever heard. But that I would never play it like that, no matter how long I practiced."

"You sell yourself short, Charlie. For a fire chief and a former mayor, you're far too modest. But I like that about you. Modesty is a fine virtue. A dying virtue, I fear, like all the other dying virtues." She placed a hand on his shoulder. "Drive safe now," she said, guiding him to the door. "Give our best to your sister, and give that lovely shepherd dog of yours a treat from me."

"Please come with me."

"Thank you for stopping, Charles," Stanley said. "You're a good neighbor. Drive carefully now. There's liable to be a lot of traffic once you get down to the highway."

"What will I say to Cathy?"

"Catherine has everything she needs. You can tell her that," said Margaret. "Tell her we said she has everything she needs. She knows that, but now and then we all need to be reminded."

Charles stood in the doorway for a moment, looking up at the mountain, now mostly obscured. The sunlight, which had filtered through the smoky air all morning, had now grown dim. How long before the flames topped the ridge and raced down the mountainside? Alas and alack, not long at all now. I might have found a way to tell them, if I wished. Such insight is within my purview. But they seemed to already know. My invisible presence brought Margaret and Stanley the peace they needed. And now I passed a bit of it on to Charles.

"Mrs. Reynolds," he said, "surely a world with something so beautiful as Chopin's Nocturnes in it has some virtue, some beauty that yet remains."

"I like the way your mind works, Charlie. It's a noble mind. The beauty in this world is indeed sublime. I and people like Father Tim would say it's a divine gift. You and Stan, you might disagree with that, but we see it, we sense the beauty, don't we? And what makes it beautiful, Charlie, is that it's fleeting. When the flower blooms, we admire it all the more because it will soon fade. Part of the pleasure we take in it comes from our knowledge of that. And therefore we can't separate the joy from the sadness: they are one in the same. We savor the beauty even as we grieve its loss."

"Mrs. Reynolds . . ."

"We'll meet again, Charlie. You needn't worry. You take care, young man."

He stepped out on the porch and took a moment to compose himself. He climbed into his truck, jotted something into a notebook, and drove slowly down the driveway, over the bridge, and made the turn out onto the main road.

A FEW HOURS later, Margaret and Stanley sat at the kitchen table. Through the window they could now see tall flames visible up at the ridgeline, glowing red-orange and spitting energy into the dark sky. And the wind was now roaring as it swept down the mountainside, filled with swirling ash and heat and righteous anger. The window shook in its casement. The wind chimes beat against the siding. The rain gutter broke off and dangled from the edge of the roof.

The table was set: two rows of Valium pills had been lined up, a bottle of Prosecco and two flutes, a lit pair of tapered candles in their silver holders, a small jar of extra virgin olive oil. I had blown out the power, and the house was dark save the flicker from the candlelight.

Margaret opened her *Book of Common Prayer* and read aloud: "In sure and certain hope of the resurrection to eternal life through our Lord Jesus Christ, we commend ourselves to Almighty God, and we commit our bodies to the elements; earth to earth, ashes to ashes, dust to dust. The Lord bless us and keep us, the Lord make his face to shine upon us and be gracious to us, the Lord lift up his countenance upon us and grant us eternal peace. Amen."

Hallelujah was the word I whispered, my only vocalization during this charge. But the word was covered by the sound of the wind—a fierce, swirling, whip of a wind that shattered the kitchen window as I uttered it.

Margaret dabbed her finger in the olive oil and made the sign of the cross upon Stanley's forehead. He did the same for her.

Breathing was difficult for them now. Coughing, Stanley opened the Prosecco and filled their glasses. As they talked, they lay pills upon their tongues and sipped the wine.

"This reminds me of the sixties—washing down narcotics with bubbly," Stanley said. "Almost like we're back on the commune."

"Too bad there's no power," Margaret replied. "We could put Hendrix on the hi-fi and burn some incense."

"The burning herbs we've got," Stanley said, pointing through the broken window, "only it doesn't smell as good."

"I would never have guessed we'd end up like this," Margaret said. "When we were young the whole world was a bud about to blossom. Or so it seemed."

"Were we wrong to dream it?"

"You mean were we self-indulgent fools . . . blinded by youthful idealism and naiveté? Yes. Wrong to dream we could make a difference? No."

"Somehow now it all feels . . . I don't know, a little pointless."

Margaret frowned.

"Go ahead and say it," Stanley said.

"What?" Margaret asked.

"'O ye of little faith.' Isn't that your line now, now that we've come round once again to the subject of meaning and the nature of ultimate reality?"

"It's been almost fifty years that we've been having this argument," she said.

"*Discussion,*" he said. "We're not arguing."

"I'll tell you what—I'll just admit defeat, how's that? I'll concede to you that it *feels* pointless or that it *seems* pointless. But I still cling to the hope that it's not. That behind it all . . ."

"That's not defeat, that's compromise," he said.

"So it is. But here at the bitter end, I think you might give it to me."

"Can we call it bittersweet?"

"It is sweet that you and I still love each other after all."

The roaring wind grew louder and the air thicker. Stan opened the front door again and a gust of heat entered the house, blowing out the candles. He returned to the table. He filled their glasses with the last of the wine.

"Is it possible that the force behind this fire is love?" he asked.

"Are you mocking me?" she said.

"No. I'm just thinking out loud. I'm just wondering if maybe you've been right all along. Nothing else makes sense right now."

They each swallowed another Valium and washed it down with the wine.

Stanley asked, "Do you remember Hendrix at the Monterey Pop Festival?"

"I was sitting right next to you."

"When he lit his guitar on fire and conjured the flames. Do you remember that? It was a silly old parlor trick, but do you remember how thrilling that felt? The other kids around us thought he was some kind of a god, like he was channeling Zoroaster or something."

"Probably that was the acid."

"Of course it was the acid. But I felt then like I do now. I feel like if we go through that fire, right on into it, we'll know something we can't otherwise know."

"How ironic that it's the skeptic who ends with a beatific vision and me, the old church lady, who's left with a bitter taste in my mouth and a certain numbness in my spirit."

"I think maybe that burning monk was your vision."

She took his hand. They drank the last of the wine and sat together in the dark. "I guess the monk was the real sacrifice, not that silly plate of doves I was balancing so carefully. The glass temple and the procession— all a grand distraction. There was something the monk knew that the rest of us couldn't be bothered with. Even self-immolation wasn't enough to break us of our delusion."

"Can I make a final musical request?" he asked.

"Satie?"

He nodded. She went to the piano. He stood beside her as she played *Gymnopedies* until her fingers and her memory gave out. The song could barely be heard, but I granted them that final shared pleasure. It was within my purview.

Then they walked to the door and stepped out onto the porch. The roar filled their ears. The hot wind began to singe their faces. Flames leapt from the wooden bridge. It hurt terribly to breathe now as they began to suffocate.

Through the din and through the murky swirling air, a buck made its way down through the thicket on the other side of the creek. His flanks were blackened. He stepped into the creek. He lowered his head to drink and then raised it, turning from side to side to observe the chaos that had overcome the forest. His eyes fell upon Stanley and Margaret. He lowered his head again and drank.

The time for words had passed. The moment of purgation had arrived. A huge ember sailed down the mountain and landed on the roof. It smoldered there for a moment, then sparked up and became flame. The monk toppled. Hendrix conjured fiery tongues. Alas and alack. The house was ablaze. Chopin's fingers danced across the keys. Hosanna and hallelujah.

Their final thoughts were focused as prayers on behalf of their daughter, Catherine, whom I drew out into the backyard of her home in the valley many miles below. She felt a shudder; a burning sensation began in her abdomen, rose to her chest and throat; it flushed her cheeks as she watched the distant smoke. In a flash she glimpsed the light and the beauty and the love that had been freely given. For an instant, she was filled with gratitude and wonder. It was within my purview to grant this.

Then like a knife came the grief. Oh, to feel as humans feel—the ecstasy and the terror, the laughter and the emptiness! Through the kitchen window, Catherine's husband and son saw her fall to her knees in the grass, and they ran to comfort her.

Acknowledgments

The author is grateful to the editors of the following journals, where some of these stories first appeared:

Catamaran Literary Reader: "Gauguin's Razor" and "Leaf, Flower, Boll"

Narrative Magazine: "Sometimes Only the Sad Songs Will Do"

Red Wheelbarrow: "Crawlspace" and "Monday Morning"

Still Point Arts Quarterly: "Moss Beach"

Stoneboat: "Deeper Blue" and "Less Rattle, More Hum"

West Trade Review: "All the Big Jerks Who Rule the World"

ABOUT THE AUTHOR

DAVID DENNY is the author of the poetry collection *Some Divine Commotion* and a previous short story collection, *The Gill Man in Purgatory*, both from Shanti Arts. Earlier books include the poetry collections *Man Overboard* and *Fool in the Attic*. His poetry and fiction have appeared in numerous journals and magazines, including *The Sun*, *Narrative*, *Catamaran*, *Rattle*, and *Parabola*. He holds an M.F.A. degree from the University of Oregon and an M.A.T. from Fuller Theological Seminary. Awards and honors include The Thomas Merton Poetry of the Sacred Contest, The Steve Kowit Poetry Prize, The Center for Book Arts Broadside Award, an Artist Laureate Award from the Silicon Valley Arts Council, numerous Pushcart Prize nominations, and inaugural Poet Laureate of Cupertino, California. He lives in Silicon Valley where, in addition to writing, he enjoys the dual identity of Professor at De Anza College and Chaplain at Sunny View Retirement Community. What spare time he has is spent painting, hiking, and traveling with his wife, Jill, a prominent choral conductor.

SHANTI ARTS

NATURE ▪ ART ▪ SPIRIT

Please visit us online
to browse our entire book catalog,
including poetry collections and fiction,
books on travel, nature, healing, art,
photography, and more.

Also take a look at our highly
regarded art and literary journal,
Still Point Arts Quarterly, which
may be downloaded for free.

www.shantiarts.com

www.ingramcontent.com/pod-product-compliance
Lightning Source LLC
Chambersburg PA
CBHW070752180626
46818CB00007B/3081